"We have

Grasping her, he [...] feet and guid[...] garage. After stepping into the small windowless space, he closed the door behind them, effectively shutting out the smoke and smell.

Brooklyn gulped several breaths of air. "Smoke bombs."

"Yeah. I figured that was what it was when I smelled it." He glanced from his silver SUV to his black Mustang. The Jeep could go off-road if needed, but the Mustang could go faster. He quickly guided her to the sports car. "We need to get out of here in case he follows the smoke bomb with an actual bomb. Call 911 while I drive."

She climbed into the car's passenger side and had her phone to her ear before he'd even opened the driver's-side door. Landon pressed the button to lift the garage door, revved the engine and hurtled backward into the night the instant the door was high enough for his vehicle to scoot under. A bullet shattered the driver's-side window.

Chastiser had graduated from fire to guns. This meant he wouldn't have to get as close to Brooklyn to kill her. The stakes just got higher!

Rhonda Starnes is a retired middle school language arts teacher who dreamed of being a published author from the time she was in seventh grade and wrote her first short story. She lives in North Alabama with her husband, whom she lovingly refers to as Mountain Man. They enjoy traveling and spending time with their children and grandchildren. Rhonda writes heart-and-soul suspense with rugged heroes and feisty heroines.

Books by Rhonda Starnes

Love Inspired Suspense

Rocky Mountain Revenge
Perilous Wilderness Escape
Tracked Through the Mountains
Abducted at Christmas
Uncovering Colorado Secrets
Cold Case Mountain Murder
Smoky Mountain Escape
In a Killer's Crosshairs

Visit the Author Profile page at LoveInspired.com.

IN A KILLER'S CROSSHAIRS

RHONDA STARNES

LOVE INSPIRED SUSPENSE
INSPIRATIONAL ROMANCE

LOVE INSPIRED® SUSPENSE
INSPIRATIONAL ROMANCE

ISBN-13: 978-1-335-95726-9

In a Killer's Crosshairs

Copyright © 2025 by Rhonda L. Starnes

Love Inspired
22 Adelaide St. West, 41st Floor
Toronto, Ontario M5H 4E3, Canada
www.LoveInspired.com

Printed in Lithuania

O love the Lord, all ye his saints:
for the Lord preserveth the faithful,
and plentifully rewardeth the proud doer.
—*Psalm* 31:23

To Doreen. No matter how many years or miles separate us, whenever we get together, we're those same middle school girls who shared secrets and a friendship that would last a lifetime. I love you dear friend. Thank you for being one of my biggest cheerleaders.

ONE

Caught somewhere between consciousness and sleep, Brooklyn Thomas coughed and rubbed her eyes. Why was her throat so dry? She kicked off the covers. And why was she sweating? Hadn't she turned down the heat before going to bed? Even with the cooler October temperatures, she preferred setting the thermostat to sixty-six degrees overnight.

Rolling over, she reached out her hand for the glass of water on her nightstand. She groped, stretching as far as she could, but her hand did not connect with the glass.

The smell of smoke filled her nostrils, and she jerked fully awake. Bolting upright, she swung her feet to the floor and reached for the lamp on the nightstand. Brooklyn twisted the tiny knob, but the light did not come on. She twisted again. *Click. Click.* Had the bulb blown? Coughing, she rapidly blinked her eyes and willed them to adjust to the dark. There was so much smoke. Why hadn't the smoke alarm awakened her?

Because of her intense fear of burning to death in a fire, she had multiple smoke detectors on both floors of her home. She glanced at the wall. The familiar glow of the green light on the detector in her room wasn't there. Panic welled inside her. The battery couldn't be dead. She changed it twice a year when clocks rolled forward and backward.

She reached for her phone. It was gone! Hadn't she placed it on the charger when she went to bed? She always kept her phone on the nightstand.

Drawn to the faint glow of the night-light she kept plugged into the wall outlet just inside the bathroom, she sprang out of bed and walked across the carpeted floor. About three feet from her destination, she stepped in a wet puddle. Jumping back, her foot connected with the glass. Had she knocked it off the nightstand in her sleep? Was her cell phone on the floor also? She made her way to the bathroom, pushed the door wide, reached inside and clicked on the light. Then inhaled sharply. Her chest tightened as her heart skipped a beat.

Written on the mirror—with her favorite mauve lipstick—were the words *You won't escape this time!* In the lower right corner, written in black eyeliner, was *Let not sin therefore reign in your mortal body, that ye should obey it in the lusts thereof. Romans 6:12.*

Chastiser had found her! Brooklyn's worst nightmare had been realized. Despite a name change and a new lifestyle, the serial killer she'd barely escaped fifteen years ago had found her. And he'd been in her room while she slept.

She spun, expecting to find him standing behind her. Of course, he wasn't there. He wouldn't risk dying in his own blazing fire.

Smoke billowed under her closed bedroom door. Her eyes lit upon the water glass lying on the floor. Where was her cell phone? With trembling legs, she crossed to the overhead light switch on the wall to the right of her bedroom door. As she drew near, the smoke sent her into a fit of coughing. She flipped on the switch. Light flooded the room.

Covering her mouth with both hands, she dropped to the floor. Crawling, using her elbows and her knees, she searched for her phone. It was nowhere to be found. Not under her bed. Not behind the nightstand. Or anywhere else on the floor.

She had to get out of the house. Racing back toward the door, she reached out her hand, halting inches from the doorknob. Intense heat radiated off it. Rushing to the bathroom, she opened the cabinet and took out two hand towels.

After tying the ends of one cloth behind her head so it formed a mask around her mouth and nose, she headed back to the door, prepared to use the other towel as a makeshift oven mitt. As she reached for the knob a second time, a scene from a movie about firefighters she'd watched long ago flashed in her mind. When they'd opened doors, the rush of oxygen caused the fire to burst through the opening. She didn't know if that was a risk in this situation, but the smoke and intense heat warned her it would be dangerous to exit through the door.

Backing away, she turned and ran into the bathroom, then quickly soaked a couple of bath towels. She rushed to the door, shoved them against the bottom where the smoke seeped inside, then hurried to the window, overlooking the backyard. Her bedroom was on the second floor. It would be a long drop, and there was nothing below to break her fall. Unless… Could she climb down the big oak tree? She had no choice but to try. Once she was outside, she could run to the Horton farm a half-mile away.

What if Chastiser was outside waiting for her? She shook that thought out of her head. If he was hiding out there, watching to make sure she perished this time, she would deal with him after she made it out alive. He'd be in for a surprise when he found out she wasn't the same young, naive girl he had almost murdered fifteen years ago.

Brooklyn would fight for her life, as she wished she had the last time. If FBI Agent Lillian Thomas hadn't saved her... *Don't go there, Brooklyn.* Lillian *had* been there. For fourteen years, from the time she rescued Brooklyn when she was seventeen until Lillian's death last year, Lillian had been a mother figure to Brooklyn. She had even offered Brooklyn her last name when it had been decided Brooklyn should legally change hers so Chastiser would have a harder time finding her. She would not disrespect Lillian's memory by cowering this time.

Brooklyn shoved her feet into the athletic shoes she'd kicked off at the end of the bed the night before. Then, without taking time to tie the laces, she crossed to the window, unlatched the sash and pushed upward. It didn't budge. She tried once more. It would not move. She examined the window sash. He had nailed it shut.

Sweat ran down her neck, and the puckered skin of the scar on her left shoulder stung with phantom pains from the past. She glanced behind her. Flames were eating through the door. Why weren't any of her smoke alarms going off? For the same reason, her cell phone was missing. Chastiser intended to prevent her escape.

Breaking the window was her only way out, but what could she use? Her eyes lit upon her bedside lamp. The base was solid walnut, but would it be heavy enough to break the window? Crossing to the nightstand, she yanked the cord to pull the plug out of the outlet and grasped the lamp, her mouth dropping open when she saw there was no light bulb. Of course. He had removed it so she would go toward the night-light in the bathroom and see the message he'd written on the mirror.

Puffing out a breath, Brooklyn threw the lamp at the window as hard as she could. The glass cracked, and the lamp bounced backward, landing on the floor at her feet.

The bedroom and bathroom lights went out, blanketing her in darkness. The eerie glow of the fire eating through the door taunted her. Nausea welled up inside her and sweat beaded her hairline. She was going to be sick. *Air.* She needed air. Picking up the lamp, she gripped it with both hands and swung it like a club. The shattered glass broke free and tumbled onto the roof.

Spurred onward, she swung again and again until she had removed all the shards of glass. She pushed her upper body through the opening and gulped a big breath of air… and smoke. Her lungs burned, and her eyes watered.

The early-morning sky had begun to lighten. But sunrise was at least forty minutes away. Brooklyn scanned the yard, looking for a shadow figure. A crashing sound behind her caused her to jump and bang her back against the upper half of the window. Wincing, she pulled her head back into the room and glanced over her shoulder. The fire had breached the door and was quickly making its way toward her. And the ceiling was caving in behind it.

No time to worry about the dangers she'd face outside. She had to move. Pulling her body through the window, she raced across the roof of the deck below and dived into the tree.

Landon Wentworth followed Nurse Kim through the ER ward. When she'd called him while he was on his morning run to tell him Brooklyn was in the hospital, she'd instructed him to ask for her when he arrived.

"I'm still confused about what happened to Brooklyn."

"As I told you on the phone, Ms. Thomas was found—"

"I know. Disoriented on the road in front of her home. She's in serious but stable condition," he finished for her. It wasn't his intention to be rude, but he wanted answers. He hadn't even known that Brooklyn's medical records listed him as the person to notify in case of an emergency. "Why was she disoriented?"

"It seems she escaped a house fire. She inhaled a lot of smoke." The woman paused in front of a curtained cubicle across from the nurses' station. "The doctor is trying to get her moved into an inpatient room."

"Does that mean her condition is serious?"

"It means he wants someone to observe her overnight to make sure she isn't struggling to breathe and her oxygen levels continue to improve." Nurse Kim smiled. "I'll let the doctor know you're here."

After the nurse walked away, Landon went into the small partitioned off area where Brooklyn lay in a bed with a nasal cannula providing her oxygen. Her red hair was splayed across the pillow, and her normally porcelain skin tone had a gray pallor to it.

He crossed to the bed and picked up her hand. Shocked at the icy feel of it, he rubbed it between his. Brooklyn's eyelids fluttered. He squeezed her hand and leaned closer. "Brooklyn, can you hear me?"

She moaned and turned toward him, staring at him with a blank look in her eyes. The nurse needed to know she was awake. Freeing his hand, he backed away from the bedside.

Brooklyn grabbed his shirttail. "Don't leave me."

The fear etched in her blue eyes pierced his heart. He sat on the edge of the bed and brushed a strand of hair out of her face, his thumb caressing her cheek. "It's okay. You're safe."

A tear leaked out of the corner of her eye, slid down her cheek and onto his hand. In that instant, he knew, no matter what he'd believed before, she *was* family. Working together the past year to build Lillian's Legacy—a foundation he and Brooklyn had started as an extension of his aunt's private investigative business, which they'd co-inherited—had cemented their friendship. And he would put his life on the line to save her. Not because she'd meant something to his aunt, but because she meant something to him. Everyone needed people they could depend on. Even if they weren't related by blood, friends could become family.

And, since the passing of his aunt, close friendships would be all Landon ever had. He'd decided long ago it wouldn't be wise for him to desire a wife or children. After all, how could he hope to be a good husband or decent role model for children with his broken childhood? His dad—Landon's most important male role model—had been anything but nurturing. But he and Brooklyn could be honorary family.

He glanced down and saw that she'd fallen back asleep. Coaxing his hand free, he stood and crossed to the metal and plastic chair that sat nearby. The nurse had said Brooklyn escaped a house fire. Had the wiring in the old house caused a short? He'd witnessed the entryway light flickering when he'd dropped off some papers at her house a few months back and had suggested she have an electrician check the wiring. Why hadn't she heeded his advice?

Brooklyn tossed her head from one side to the other, mumbling. He stood and leaned close, turning his ear to listen. "He found me…going to die… No!" she screamed.

Landon bolted upright and stared down at her, their

gazes locking. Who had found her? It couldn't be… "Chastiser?"

Her face blanched, and she burst into tears. He sank onto the side of the bed and tried to console her, but her wails increased.

A doctor burst into the room, followed by Nurse Kim. "What's going on in here?"

"I don't know." A helpless feeling washed over him as he moved out of the way so the medical professionals could work. "She was mumbling in her sleep, then screamed and started crying."

"She's been having hysterical outbursts since her arrival. Most likely the trauma of being caught in a house fire." Nurse Kim held up a syringe. "This sedative should help."

You have no idea how traumatizing being trapped in a fire would be for her. Landon did, though. He'd heard the stories of how his aunt had rescued Brooklyn from the burning wooden box Chastiser had left her in—tied up and alive. If Lillian hadn't caught a glimpse of a taillight on a vehicle in the woods and investigated, Brooklyn would have been the killer's third victim. Chastiser had gotten away, but Lillian had put out the fire and freed Brooklyn from the homemade casket.

The nurse whispered soothing words to Brooklyn as she administered the sedative. After the doctor looked at Brooklyn's vitals on the monitor beside the bed, he turned to Landon. "I'm Dr. Yates. We need to keep her overnight to administer oxygen and monitor her CO_2 levels. She will be transferred to a room on the fourth floor within the hour."

"Thank you."

The doctor and nurse left the small cubicle. Several long minutes passed, and Landon cautiously stepped closer to the bed. Questions raced around in his head, but he had no desire to upset Brooklyn now that she'd stopped wailing. Once the hospital discharged her, there would be time to discuss what had happened.

The chair squeaked when he settled into it. She turned her head in his direction. He leaned forward, his elbows on his knees. The sad expression on her face gutted him. He'd never seen her look so completely lost.

"He locked me in…thought I would die…" she mumbled. "Climbed out… He burst out of the shadows…saw head-lights…ran…so hard…" Yawning, she closed her eyes. A few minutes later, a soft snore escaped. The sedative had kicked in.

Settling against the back of the chair, he absorbed her words. Had someone set fire to her house? Or was she confusing old memories with current events? He'd have to wait until the sedative wore off before he could get answers.

An hour later, he paced the hall on the fourth floor as the nurses settled Brooklyn into her room. He hadn't wanted to leave her side until he determined if the fire had been an attempt on her life or not. But the nurses had insisted they needed to assist a still-groggy Brooklyn out of her smoke-infused pajamas and into a hospital gown.

Landon was on his third trek past Brooklyn's room when he looked up and saw Sheriff Heath Dalton striding toward him. "I'm surprised to see you here, Sheriff. Isn't this outside your jurisdiction?"

"It is, but I wanted to come by and check on Brooklyn."

"That was nice of you." Landon furrowed his brow. "I didn't realize you and Brooklyn were such good friends."

The sheriff pinned him with a quizzical expression. "My *wife*, Kayla, and I think highly of Brooklyn. She sits behind us at church every week. But this isn't a social call. I've just come from the crime scene at her house, and I have a few questions for her."

Crime scene? So, Brooklyn had been talking about the fire this morning and not the time she escaped Chastiser's attempt on her life. "What happened?"

"There was a fire. The best we can piece together, Brooklyn busted out her bedroom window and climbed down a tree. Thankfully, Sue Griffin was on her way to open the diner when Brooklyn ran into the road. She stopped and got Brooklyn into her vehicle. Then she called 911 to report the fire and drove Brooklyn to the EMS station to be checked out. They transported her here."

"You said it was a crime scene?"

"We'll have to wait for the official report from the fire investigator," Heath said. "But according to Chief Butler, all signs point to arson."

The words hit Landon like a bucket of ice water. Who would want to kill his business partner—a psychologist whose sole goal in life was to save as many women as she could from a life on the streets? Did the person responsible know Brooklyn's greatest fear was being burned alive? No, they wouldn't know that. His Aunt Lillian had worked diligently to protect Brooklyn's history, even helping Brooklyn legally change her own name so no one would associate her with the serial killer who had almost killed her. Unless... Could it be? "Your officers should search the crime scene for a Bible verse."

Heath narrowed his eyes. "Do you know who did this?"

"You already found the verse, didn't you?" Landon demanded.

"Yes. There may have been two of them. Chief Butler said it looked like someone had written a message on her bathroom mirror with lipstick, but the heat from the fire had made it illegible."

"The other one?" Landon prompted.

"It was spray-painted on the side of her SUV."

"What did it say?"

"'But every man is tempted, when he is drawn away of his own lust, and enticed,'" Heath recited.

"James 1:14," they said in unison.

"I need to see Brooklyn. Now!" Landon moved to go around Heath, and the sheriff put out a hand to halt him. He shrugged him off and barreled into Brooklyn's room—startling the two nurses on their way out.

He stepped aside and allowed the women to pass. After the nurses had exited the room, he turned his attention to Brooklyn.

Heath entered the room behind him, closing the door. "Who do you think is behind the fire?"

Landon locked gazes with Brooklyn and strolled toward her. "Chastiser."

"The serial killer?" Heath asked. "It's been more than twelve years since his last murder. Why would you think it's him?"

"Because it *was* him." Silent tears slipped down Brooklyn's cheeks. "He left a message on my bathroom mirror."

"But he put his victims in wooden crates, almost like caskets." Heath moved to the other side of the hospital bed. "I never heard of him setting fire to a house with his victim inside. Wouldn't it be more likely that this was someone else?"

"Possibly, except... As far as we know, I'm Chastiser's only victim who got out alive."

Shock registered on Heath's face. "What? Chastiser attempted to kill you before? Why have I never heard of this?"

"When it happened, my aunt worked hard to keep it out of the media." Landon turned to the sheriff. "Brooklyn wanted a fresh start—to put all that she went through behind her."

"If it is Chastiser, this investigation will fall under the FBI's jurisdiction. I'll have to notify them."

Landon nodded. Aunt Lillian had been an FBI agent for thirty years, and he'd been an agent for twelve years before walking away last year to run his aunt's company and honor her legacy, so he understood protocol better than most civilians. "I expect Jackson Knight is the agent you'll talk to, since he's the special agent in charge at the Knoxville office. Ask him to call me as soon as he gets a chance. Also, please, do everything you can to protect Brooklyn's identity."

"That goes without saying." Heath pulled out his cell phone and slipped from the room.

Landon picked up Brooklyn's hand, rubbing his thumb over the back of it. "We will catch him this time. I won't let him hurt you again."

She nodded, pulled her hand free and rolled over, turning her back to him.

He wanted to demand she talk to him—trust him to keep his word. But he knew better than to force the issue. Even though Aunt Lillian had not raised Brooklyn from childhood, like she'd raised him, Brooklyn had lived in Lillian's home for six years while earning her high school equivalency and her bachelor's degree. But he and Brooklyn had never lived in Lillian's home together. Landon had been a senior at Duke University when Brooklyn moved in, and although he came home during school breaks, he and Brooklyn had not developed a familial bond at that time. He had often suspected their time in Lillian's home not overlapping for long periods of time had been a good thing. They had been cordial with each other on the rare family holiday, but their personalities were so different he imagined they would have clashed like cats and dogs if they had grown up together, just like a real brother and sister.

Brooklyn was more reserved—closed off. She craved privacy and did not share her thoughts or her personal space. Landon believed if someone wanted better out of life, they had to charge ahead and not be afraid to take chances. He never wanted his negative experiences to stop him from achieving his dreams. And making his aunt proud—even now when she was no longer here to celebrate his accomplishments with him—would always be important to him. She might not have given birth to him, but she had been, for all intents and purposes, his mom.

When he was seven years old, his father had driven him to school one morning then returned home to murder Landon's mom before committing suicide. Aunt Lillian—his mom's fourteen-years-older, never-married sister—had taken him from San Diego to live with her in Knoxville, Tennessee. He had wallowed in a pit of sadness after losing his parents, thinking no one could understand what he was going through and frustrated at his inability to fully express his thoughts and feelings. But Aunt Lillian had been a unique and patient person. Though she had been a full-time working guardian with a demanding job, Landon never felt alone. To the best of her ability, she had arranged her schedule so she was home each evening in time for dinner and to help him with his homework. And when he'd gotten older and involved in sports, she'd prioritized attending as many games as she could.

That was why, when she passed away last year, he'd left his career with the FBI to run the private investigative business she had started after rescuing Brooklyn from Chastiser. It wouldn't surprise him to discover that she had been the one who encouraged Brooklyn to update her medical records, ensuring that he would be informed in case of an emergency.

Aunt Lillian had loved Brooklyn like a daughter, which was why he would do everything in his power to protect her. Landon would finish what his aunt had started. He would protect Brooklyn, and he would do whatever it took to stop Chastiser once and for all.

TWO

Brooklyn frowned, picked up the fork and pushed the mushy scrambled eggs around the plate. Forking a small amount, she cautiously took a bite. Yuck. She dropped the silverware, and it clattered onto the tray. Then she picked up the bacon and took a bite. At least it was crispy and hadn't been burned. She never would understand why hospital food always tasted so bland. Of course, she didn't have an appetite, so it didn't matter what the eggs tasted like.

Picking up the small glass of orange juice, she gulped it then settled the glass onto the tray with a sigh.

"Why such a heavy sigh?" Landon asked as he walked into the room with a shopping bag from a local outlet mall looped on his arm and a tray with two cups from her favorite coffee shop in his hand. He placed the bag on the chair beside her bed. Then he removed a cup from the takeout tray and held it out to her. "Caramel macchiato."

"Thank you." She accepted the cup. "You don't have any food in that bag, do you?"

"You're welcome. And no, sorry. I didn't bring food." He eyed her plate. "But I promise to get you whatever you'd like to eat after you're discharged."

She appreciated his thoughtfulness. "The doctor was in earlier. He said he'd complete my paperwork after he finished his rounds. I should be out of here in a couple of hours. Agent Knight stopped by also. He wanted to know everything that happened. I don't think he's ready to believe Chastiser set the fire."

"The FBI can't take your word for it, especially since you didn't see him."

"Even if I had seen him, I wouldn't be able to identify him. Chastiser wears a mask and a wig." An image of the man in a red clown wig and a gas mask who'd abducted her fifteen years ago flashed through her mind, and she shivered. Popping the lid off her coffee, she inhaled deeply.

"I asked Agent Knight how badly the fire damaged my home. He refused to answer. I guess he didn't want to be the one to break the bad news to me." She met Landon's eyes. "I no longer have a home to go back to, do I?"

He set his coffee on the rolling table at the foot of her bed, then sank onto the mattress beside her and picked up her hand. "I don't want you worrying about any of that. Your home can be replaced. Right now, we are going to be thankful that you got out alive."

"This time," she whispered. "But how many more times can I escape him?"

Landon squeezed her hand. "I will make sure you're not put into a situation where you have to escape him again."

"How are you going to do that?"

"You're going to move in with me until he's captured."

"What? I can't do that."

"Yes, you can," he said forcefully. "I've already discussed it with Agent Knight. With my experience and training as an agent, we feel like it's the safest place for you. *And*, he agreed this case has several markings to indicate Chastiser is behind the attack—especially given your history with him—*but*, until he can prove that it *is* Chastiser, he won't be able to obtain the authorization to send you to a safe house."

"I wouldn't go even if he could." She pulled her hand free from Landon's. Why was he coddling her? He'd never been touchy-feely with her before. "I have clients to see—women who need to get out of the situations they've found themselves in. They shouldn't be forced to stay trapped in their current state because of me."

Brooklyn understood the conditions most of her clients lived in. As a runaway teen, she'd been drugged and trafficked by someone she'd thought loved her. She'd learned harsh realities about life and about her inability to judge people's true character, especially when it came to men, which was why she'd dedicated her life to saving other women who had been tricked and used just like she had been.

"You can't help anyone if you're dead," Landon said firmly.

"I agree." Brooklyn closed her eyes, took a deep breath, puffed it out slowly then looked up. "Which is why I will accept your offer to stay with you until I can make further arrangements. However, since our offices are in your home, I will continue to see clients and potential clients who come my way."

"But—"

"I'm not backing down on this point. It's too important." She locked gazes with him, daring him to argue with her.

"Why do you have to be so hardheaded?" Landon asked.

Brooklyn shrugged. "Probably for the same reason you are. We were both influenced by a fiercely determined woman who never backed down when she felt strongly about something."

You have every right to wallow in self-pity and hide from

the world after what you've been through, but I'll be dis-
appointed if you do. I thought you had more grit than that.
Lillian's words echoed in the far chambers of her mind.
Brooklyn had stayed in the hospital for seventeen days after
her first near-death encounter with Chastiser. She'd suffered from smoke inhalation and second and third-degree
burns on her left side, including her shoulder and upper
back. Lillian had been her only visitor during her hospital
stay—coming to see her almost daily. Once Brooklyn had
been discharged, Lillian had offered her home as a place
for Brooklyn's continued recovery.

Brooklyn hadn't been sure what she'd expected from the
tough-as-nails woman she'd later learned was a retired federal agent, but Lillian hadn't coddled her or tried to comfort
her when she'd been weepy. Instead, Lillian had showered
Brooklyn with tough love, instilling in her the determina-
tion to have a better life and not let Chastiser consume her
mind. Brooklyn would carry those lessons with her until
the day she died. And she would not allow Chastiser to win
by causing her to hide in fear.

Landon moved the bags in his right hand to his left and
sifted through the keys on his key ring. When he located
the correct one, he inserted it into the lock and twisted.

"I could take some of those bags," Brooklyn said.

"No need. I've got them." He pushed open the door that
led from the garage into the kitchen, stepped back and allowed her to enter ahead of him. "You know the code for
the alarm."

She nodded and punched in the code to shut off the alarm
before it could sound. Then she stepped into the kitchen
and deposited the fast-food restaurant bag on the table. He
followed behind, pushing the door closed.

After leaving the hospital, they had stopped at a national chain retail store so she could pick up necessities—pajamas, toiletries, a couple of changes of clothes—and replace her cell phone, which they'd discovered had last pinged on I-140 at the Tennessee River bridge. It seemed Chastiser might have thrown the phone into the river. Landon had also gifted her with a discreet-looking smart watch with its own cell service and had asked her to temporarily allow him to turn on the feature that would share her location with him. Afraid of Chastiser abducting her again, she'd readily agreed. Although she didn't plan to get far from Landon's sight until this ordeal was over.

"I'm sorry we didn't have time to swing by your house before nightfall. We'll go in the morning. Okay?"

"I have an appointment at nine with Tiffany Carmichael. You met her, remember?"

"Petite nineteen-year-old with bleached blond hair and a huge chip on her shoulder. Is she the one who was arrested for drugs and…um…soliciting companionship?"

"Yes." Brooklyn frowned. "I've met with her twice weekly since she was released from jail eight weeks ago. The judge made counseling a condition of her probation. He's sent several young women to me. Some are successful, and others end up back in jail."

"How does everything seem to be going with Tiffany?"

"She has a four-month-old daughter. The baby was born with drugs in her system and taken by social services after birth. Tiffany's mom has temporary custody. But all Tiffany can talk about are the things she's going to do for Jasmine and the kind of childhood she's going to give her daughter when she gets her back. When we met four days ago, I thought Tiffany was ready to go to rehab, so she could work toward getting her baby back. But it's obvious that she fears her *boyfriend*—the guy giving her the drugs and pushing her to…um…"

"I get it. Is he the dad of her baby?"

"He's denying paternity and refused to allow her to put his name on the birth certificate. Given her lifestyle, it's likely he isn't the father."

"How many counseling sessions did the judge order?"

"Twenty total. I only have four more chances to make her realize she doesn't have to stay trapped in her current lifestyle."

Brooklyn's insistence that she had to continue to work despite Chastiser reappearing in her life made sense now. She would not want to jeopardize the progress she'd made with Tiffany, especially if she thought she was close to convincing the young woman to take a chance on a better life.

"My counseling sessions only last an hour. I can be ready to go see what's left of my home at ten, if that works for you."

"I can make that work." He nodded to the alarm keypad and held up the bags he carried. "Reset the alarm while I take these to your room."

Brooklyn moved to do as he asked, and he headed up the back stairs, taking them two at a time. Entering Brooklyn's room, he placed the bags on the bed, then laughed. It hadn't occurred to him that he'd subconsciously thought of the room as hers and not as a guest room. But that's what Aunt Lillian had called it—Brooklyn's room—from the first day seventeen-year-old Brooklyn had entered the home fifteen years ago.

Wanting her former ward to have a place to return to that felt like home, Lillian had left the room the way Brooklyn had decorated it, even after she'd moved out to attend graduate school. Lillian had done the same with Landon's room, too. However, after he'd returned to Knoxville to run the private investigation agency, he had moved all of his things into the master bedroom and converted his childhood room into a home gym.

Lillian had run her agency out of her home. She had converted most of the downstairs—the library, formal living room and dining room—into office spaces for her and Brooklyn, who had joined Lillian's agency after completing her graduate degree, but had left the eat-in kitchen and small gathering room as living spaces. The setup had worked well, but it was time to find a new office space.

In her will, Lillian had left Landon her home and sixty percent ownership in the agency, bequeathing Brooklyn the other forty percent ownership. In the year since they had taken over the responsibilities of the business, they had also started the nonprofit, Lillian's Legacy, as a way to provide services to people in need who could not afford to hire them.

He smiled, thinking about turning the entire house back into a home. When he'd joined the FBI, he'd purchased a small condo—not believing that a bachelor needed much more than a place to lay his head and cook a few meals, especially since he'd never marry. But since returning to Knoxville, he'd realized how much he had missed living in his aunt's house. The old Victorian built in the late 1800s with its creaky floors and large backyard felt like an old friend who always knew how to make his days brighter.

"What's taking so long?" Brooklyn yelled. "The food's getting cold."

"Coming." A cold hamburger wouldn't be too bad, but cold fries were another matter. He raced down the stairs.

Brooklyn had set the table with plates from the cabinet and poured them each a glass of sweet tea.

"Thank you for doing this." He settled into a chair. "But you shouldn't have gone to so much trouble. I would've been fine eating out of the paper wrappers."

"Lillian always insisted on using the place settings appropriate for every meal. In this case, a plate and napkins." She grinned. "If you'd bought pizza, I might have used her fine china."

He laughed. "You're right. I had forgotten. Guess I spent too many years living away from her..." His voice cracked and he swallowed past the lump that had settled in his throat. Aunt Lillian had been his mom for more years than his biological mother had, yet he had failed to visit her regularly. He would give anything to have one more day with her.

"I miss her, too," Brooklyn whispered. "She was an amazing lady."

"Yes, she was. I regret being so wrapped up in my career that I didn't take the time to visit as often as I should have."

"She was proud of you for following in her footsteps and becoming an agent. She always bragged about the cases you solved and told everyone how successful you were."

"I tried to call her at least once a week." His comment sounded pathetic, even to his ears—an excuse for his lack of care for his aunt in her later years.

He cleared his throat. "I owe you an apology."

"For?"

"For pushing you to do the television interview. If that's how Chastiser found you, I don't know that I will ever forgive myself."

"Why? I'm a grown woman. Sure, you *encouraged* me to do the interview, but I could've said no. *And* it was supposed to just be a local newscast. How would you know a national news outlet would pick it up?"

"Yes, but—"

"Besides, we don't even know if that's how he found me."

Landon raised an eyebrow. "I don't believe in coincidences. You did the interview discussing the work we're doing at Lillian's Legacy a week ago. It hit national news the next day. Five days later, you're attacked by Chastiser."

"Yes, but I look nothing like I did at seventeen. My teeth are straighter. My hair is darker. Not to mention, my skin is clearer. Plus, my name is different, *and* I didn't mention my previous encounter with Chastiser in the interview."

"No, but you mentioned your life prior to the attack and that Lillian rescued you and gave you a fresh start."

"Well, what's done is done. All we can do now is pray we catch him before he has another chance to kill me."

She was right. One thing he had always admired about Brooklyn was her no-nonsense manner. He also knew that her personality would keep her from hiding from the serial killer. She would want to go on with life as normal. He doubted that decision would be a good one, which meant it was up to him to keep her safe.

THREE

Brooklyn picked up her desk phone and pressed the intercom button. "Any news from Tiffany?"

"No, ma'am," Marianne Vaughn, the secretary, replied.

"It isn't like her to be late."

"Do you want me to call her again?"

Brooklyn shook her head even though Marianne couldn't see her. "No. You've already tried twice."

"Okay. I have to go to the post office and the bank. Do you need anything else while I'm out?"

"No. But Landon and I will most likely be gone before you return. Let Dana know that she'll have to handle everything until you get back. We'll deal with anything that needs our attention when we return. Also, since we're not expecting any deliveries or clients for the rest of the day, it's probably best to leave the doors locked and the alarm activated."

"Yes, ma'am."

Disconnecting the call, Brooklyn drummed her fingers on her desk. The receptionist, Dana Reed, had only worked for them for three weeks and had never had to deal with everything alone. Brooklyn furrowed her brow then glanced at the large clock on the wall opposite her desk. It was 9:20 a.m.

She sighed. Dana would be fine. She'd only be here alone for an hour, max.

Standing, Brooklyn crossed to the door that separated her office from Landon's. She rapped on the mahogany wood.

"Come in."

Sliding the pocket door open, she stepped into his office. "Tiffany is a no-show, so I'm ready to leave whenever you are."

Landon looked up from his laptop. "I just need to finish this email. Only two more sentences." His fingers flew across the keys. "Okay. I'm done. Let's go." He closed his laptop, stood and crossed to the door to the hallway. She followed close behind as he led the way through the kitchen and into the garage.

Settling into the passenger seat of his Jeep, she could not get her mind off Tiffany. Had something happened to the young woman? Could she have been in an accident? Tiffany knew how important these sessions were. Once Brooklyn reported her missed appointment to the court, the judge could revoke her parole and send her to jail.

"You're not going to have any fingernails left if you don't stop chewing on them," Landon said as he clicked his seat belt into place. "Are you worried Chastiser will be waiting for us at your house? You know I won't let anything happen to you, right?"

"I'm worried about Tiffany. She's always on time and has never missed an appointment. Actually, she's always ten minutes early. It's one of her quirks. She doesn't like to be late. I can't believe she willingly missed today's session. I have a bad feeling about this."

"Do you know where she lives? We could swing by and check on her."

"You wouldn't mind?"

"Of course not." He pressed the button on the garage-door remote clipped on the sun visor, started the Jeep and backed out of the garage, then closed the door before backing onto the street.

"Thanks. I'll text Marianne and have her send me the address." Brooklyn quickly sent the message. "She's running errands. It will be a while before she gets back to the office and pulls up the information. We may as well go to my house first then check on Tiffany when we return."

Forty minutes later, Landon turned onto the road that led to the small farmhouse Brooklyn had purchased five years ago. Preferring a small-town vibe over the hustle and bustle of a city setting, she'd chosen to move to the community of Barton Creek. Lillian had tried to convince her to move into a condo closer to their offices, telling her a forty-five-minute commute would be unpleasant. However, the drive each day had proven to be relaxing. It gave her time to listen to her audio Bible and decompress.

Brooklyn sat up straighter as anxiety built inside her. Would any part of her home be salvageable? "Have you seen my house?"

"Yes. I came by after leaving the hospital the day you were admitted. The fire was out by the time I arrived, but the house was still smoldering."

Tears stung the back of her eyes. She clenched her jaw, desperate to stop the waterworks.

"Are you okay?"

"I know material things can be replaced, but this is gut-wrenching." Brooklyn sighed. "If I weren't about to cry, I'd laugh. I've spent my adult life trying to live a minimalistic lifestyle. While growing up in foster care, moving from place to place, I lost every childhood treasure I owned. The trinkets weren't worth two cents, but they meant the world to me because they were mine."

"It's normal to be sad. You worked hard to get where you are in life." He cast a quick glance in her direction. "How long were you in foster care?"

Too long. The various foster homes flashed through her mind. Nine in total. Some had been nicer than others, and if she were honest, she had brought on most of her struggles with her attitude. If only she'd known that, maybe she could have saved herself some of the heartache she'd endured in the foster homes that were more about collecting money than nurturing children. "Five and a half years. My stepdad died in an automobile accident when I was eight. After he died, my mom developed an alcohol problem. At age ten, I figured out I could skip school by telling her it was a holiday or that it was the weekend. She never questioned me, even if I said it was Saturday three days in a row. Eventually, the school reported me for truancy and the Department of Children's Services came to investigate. When the DCS social worker arrived, Mom was passed out on the sofa. They couldn't wake her, so they called an ambulance to transport her to the hospital and immediately removed me from the home."

"You said stepdad. What about your biological father? Where was he?"

She frowned and shook her head. "I don't know. I never even learned his name. On my birth certificate it said unknown."

"Where's your mom now?"

"Less than a year after I was removed from my home, Mom died of alcohol poisoning. When they told me, I became even more rebellious."

"You were sixteen when you ran away."

"Yeah. I had a chip on my shoulder, feeling like I didn't belong anywhere. I thought I could make a better life on my own. Didn't turn out that way."

"You may have had a few tough years, but you survived the storm. Look at you now. You're a successful psychologist, helping other young women who find themselves in a similar situation. You own your own home—"

"That Chastiser burned down."

"You have insurance, so you can rebuild. I would say you're not doing too badly."

"You have Lillian's optimism. I never realized that before."

"I'll take that as a compliment." He slowed the vehicle. "Are you ready to see the damage?"

"Honestly, no, but I have to face it sometime. So, it may as well be now."

Landon turned onto the dirt driveway leading to her home that sat back off the road. She gasped. The exterior walls remained standing. However, the roof had caved in and it was obvious the house was gutted.

"My home is gone." The tears she had fought to keep at bay streamed freely now. She was being ridiculous. It wasn't like she had family photos or priceless heirlooms from generations past, but the belongings she'd had were things she had worked hard for.

Landon reached over and squeezed her hand. "It's going to be fine. I'll help you deal with the insurance company. You can rebuild your home just the way you want it."

"What's the use? Until we catch *him*, I can't be alone or have anything nice. He'll just burn everything down again." She turned to Landon. "We have to figure out who Chastiser is so we can stop him."

"I've been thinking about that. You had to have crossed

paths with him somewhere in your life for him to target you. The only thing his victims had in common is that they didn't have family. Most of them lived on the streets."

"Yes, but I was already off the street when I became his victim. I had a job at the truck stop and the owner rented me the small apartment above her garage."

Landon put the vehicle in Park, turned off the engine and faced her. "Aunt Lillian mentioned, prior to you getting the job at the truck stop, you'd gotten mixed up with drugs and had fallen prey to traffickers. Could you have crossed paths with Chastiser during that time and he tracked you to the truck stop?"

She had never thought of that, but he was right. She had only been working at the truck stop three weeks when Chastiser abducted her and placed her in the claustrophobic wooden box he'd set on fire. Her mind reeled. She'd always thought she'd *met* Chastiser at the truck stop, but maybe not.

She opened her door and got out. There might be nothing left to salvage, but she had to at least look around. Even though what remained of her home was exposed, she headed for the porch, intent on going through the front door that no longer stood in place.

A vehicle door closed behind her, and Landon jogged over to her. "I know you want to look around, but be careful."

She nodded, lifted the yellow caution tape and stepped into the foyer, her foot crunching on broken glass in the entryway. Brooklyn made her way toward the living room. Her bed had fallen through the floor above and lay in the middle of the room. All the items in the room either had burned, melted or shattered.

"Look at this."

She turned around to see Landon holding out the antique

pewter picture frame that had sat on her mantel. The picture inside was the only photo she owned of her, Lillian and Landon together. They had snapped the photo on Thanksgiving, only three months before Lillian passed away. Having a family photo taken had been Lillian's last request. Brooklyn accepted the frame.

"The glass is broken, and the photo is covered in a layer of soot. But I have the same photo, so I can have a replacement copy made for you."

Lillian's smiling face looked up at Brooklyn, and she pulled the photo to her chest and hugged it. "I can't believe this survived." Even damaged, she'd keep this photo for the rest of her life.

"Sometimes you can find small things like that scattered, here or there, that somehow missed the damaging heat of the fire."

"I guess I'll keep digging."

Landon's phone rang, and she saw Agent Knight's name flash on the screen. He pressed the button to answer and put the phone to his ear.

"Hello." He listened, shock registering on his face before he could shutter his expression.

"What is it? What's wrong?" she whispered, clutching his arm.

"We'll meet you back at my house."

He tucked the phone into his pocket and escorted her out of the rubble. "Agent Knight wants to meet with us."

"What happened? I saw the look on your face. It's something bad, isn't it?"

Landon guided her back to his Jeep. He opened the passenger side door, but she planted her feet. "I'm not going anywhere until you tell me what happened."

He sighed. "Chastiser has claimed another victim. A fisherman found a burned wooden casket on the riverbank."

Her knees buckled. She sank into the passenger seat.

"There's more." He stooped down to look her in the eyes. "Agent Knight believes the victim is Tiffany."

"No!" A guttural cry ripped from her throat. She shook her head. "No. She's ready to leave her boyfriend and the life he forced her into. She wants to become a chef."

"He thinks Chastiser murdered her yesterday afternoon."

Brooklyn shook her head. "He could be wrong. It may not be her. There's no way there's been enough time to identify the body—not with the condition Chastiser would have left it in."

Landon placed his hand on her shoulder. "It seems Chastiser wanted *you* to know who the victim was. He left her identification and belongings at the crime scene, along with a message. For you."

A shudder ran the length of her body. "What was the message?"

"Tiffany took your place. But next time, you'll have to accept your own punishment, Hope Jennings."

Hope Jennings. The name she had left behind when she closed the door on her past. Was her time running out? Only God knew the answer. One thing was for sure, she would do everything in her power to survive and see that Chastiser answered for all the lives he had taken, especially Tiffany's.

Landon puffed out his breath as he extended his arms, lifting the bar with the 240 pounds of weight into the air before bringing it back down and resting it on the cradle. Dropping his feet to the ground, he scooched forward and sat up. Then he grabbed the hand towel off the nearby stool and mopped the sweat off his face and neck.

He checked his smart watch. It was almost ten o'clock. He hadn't heard Brooklyn come upstairs yet. Of course, he had been focused on his workout as he labored to burn off excess energy and process the details of the case. The devastated look in Brooklyn's blue eyes when she'd seen the evidence left behind by Chastiser had caused all of Landon's protective instincts to go into overdrive.

Crossing to the door, he stepped out into the hall and paused beside her door. No sound came from inside. He knocked lightly. "Brooklyn?"

No reply. Was she still in her office working? He went down the hall to the front staircase and raced down the steps. Crossing the foyer, he barged into her office without knocking.

Brooklyn jumped and looked up from her computer, placing a hand on her chest. "You startled me."

His steps faltered, and he stopped in the middle of the room.

"Sorry." He took a deep breath and slowly released it, trying to calm his heart rate. "I was worried when you weren't in your room. Shouldn't you be finished by now?"

"I was just finishing up." She clicked a few keys on the laptop, waited for it to power off and closed the lid. "All done." She turned to him. "Did you have a nice workout?"

"I don't know that a workout can be considered *nice*." He smiled. "But it felt good and helped me gain some perspective."

"Oh, how so?"

He dropped into the chair in front of her desk and leaned forward, resting his elbows on his knees. "I've decided to close our offices."

"What! No." She shook her head. "We're doing such

good work here. If you don't want to be a part of it, I'll run things alone."

"No. You don't understand what I'm saying. We're not closing permanently. However, I believe it's imperative we close temporarily."

She started to speak, and he held up a hand. "Look, I don't like it any more than you do. But we cannot put anyone else in danger. It's evident Chastiser is watching. He could target any of the young women who visit here, including our employees. We'll close for one week then reevaluate the situation. I'll have Marianne and Dana start rescheduling all our upcoming appointments tomorrow."

She puffed out a breath and slumped back in her chair. "You're right. I know you are, but it frustrates me that we're letting *him* win."

"The only way Chastiser wins is if he gets the prize he's seeking, which is *you*. I won't let that happen." He sat up straight. "In order to protect you, we have to go on the defense. By closing temporarily, we can stay a few steps ahead of him, while focusing our attention on figuring out who he is and stopping him before he kills again."

"What about our employees? I'm not sure they can afford to miss a week without pay."

She was correct. Marianne was a widowed mother of a three-year-old, and Dana was a full-time college student, attending classes four nights a week. She relied on her income to pay for food and housing. "They will still receive their pay."

"Okay. That's good, as a temporary solution. But what if we don't solve this in a week? We can't afford to stay closed indefinitely, and not just because of the monetary hit we would take. We also have to think about the people needing our services."

"I don't want you worrying about any of that right now. We'll figure everything out. We just need to take a step back and reevaluate."

She bit her lip, then nodded. "Okay."

Relief washed over him, and he pushed to his feet. "I'll check all the locks before going upstairs to change." He paused in the doorway. "Do you anticipate staying downstairs long? If you're going to continue to work, I can come back down and help you."

"No. I'm finished for the night. I plan to make a cup of hot tea then head to my room."

"Okay. Good night."

"Good night."

He quickly checked all the doors and headed upstairs, taking the steps two at a time. Ten minutes later he exited the bathroom with damp hair, wearing well-worn jeans and his favorite football jersey. A night owl by nature, it would be several hours before he was ready to turn in for the night. He opened his bedroom door and stepped into the hall, needing the reassurance that Brooklyn was safely upstairs and tucked away in her room. Once he knew she was asleep, he planned to walk the perimeter of his property to make sure nothing seemed out of place.

Lights were still on downstairs. What was taking her so long? Returning to his room, he shoved his feet into his slippers. Maybe she'd sat down and fallen asleep waiting for the tea water to heat. As he stepped back into the hall, the sound of glass breaking echoed from below, and Brooklyn's scream pierced the air.

Landon darted back into his room, snatched his Glock out of his nightstand drawer and ran to the back staircase. The smell of fireworks and smoke filled the air.

"Brooklyn!" He coughed, his eyes watering as he searched the room.

He spotted her, crouched on the floor, her arms covering her head, a spilled cup of tea nearby. Grasping her by the arm, he pulled her to her feet. "We have to go. Now!"

Landon tucked his revolver into his waistband and guided her to the door leading into the garage. Stepping into the small, windowless space, he closed the door behind them, shutting out the smoke and smell.

Brooklyn gulped several breaths of air. "Smoke bombs."

"Yeah. I figured that was what it was." He glanced from his Wrangler to his Mustang. The Jeep could go off-road if needed, but the Mustang could go faster. He quickly guided her to the sports car. "We need to get out of here in case he follows the smoke bombs with an actual bomb. Call 911 while I drive."

She climbed into the car while he ran around the front to the driver's side. Her phone was pressed to her ear before he'd even opened his door. Landon pressed the button to lift the garage door, revved the engine and hurtled backward into the night the instant the door was high enough for his vehicle to scoot under. Seconds later, a bullet shattered the driver's side window.

Chastiser had graduated from fire to guns. This meant he wouldn't have to get as close to Brooklyn to kill her. The stakes just got higher!

FOUR

Brooklyn slid down into the floorboard, her attention attuned to the voice on the other end of her phone.

"Nine-one-one. What is your emergency?"

She gave the operator the address and quickly filled her in on the situation. "He's shooting at us. Please send an officer."

More bullets hit the vehicle, followed by the sound of glass breaking. Brooklyn watched Landon as he backed into the road, shifted into gear and accelerated, the tires squealing on the pavement.

"Where are you now?" the operator asked in her ear.

Brooklyn climbed onto the seat, fastened her seat belt and placed the call on speaker. "We're in the vehicle. We were leaving the residence because the assailant threw smoke bombs into the home. As we were exiting the garage, he started shooting at us."

"I have officers en route now."

"Do you have an ETA?" Landon asked.

"Six minutes. If you've left the home, where should I tell the officers you'll be so they can question you about the incident?"

"Tell them we'll return home, but I won't stop until I see

they are on scene." He provided a description of his vehicle, including his license plate number.

The sound of laptop keys clicking came across the line. "I've relayed the message. The officers will expect you, but you should remain in your vehicle until they've secured the property."

Brooklyn disconnected the call. "Do you think Chastiser knew I was there, or do you think he attacked the offices because I mentioned the address in the interview?"

"He knew you were there," Landon stated matter-of-factly. "He only shot at the left side of the vehicle. It was obvious he was trying to take me out without hitting you."

"Couldn't it just be that the left side was closest to where he was standing?"

"When I backed into the road, the passenger side of the vehicle faced the house, and he stopped shooting until I turned and the driver's side of the vehicle was facing the house again." She glanced in his direction and saw his jaw muscle twitch. "If he didn't know you were in the vehicle with me, he would have shot at either side of the vehicle."

She closed her eyes. "If he kills the person he sees as my protector, it would be easier to take me and torture me the same way he does all of his victims."

"That would be my summation."

Wrapping her arms tightly around her middle, she tried to quell the anxiety and nausea threatening to overtake her.

"Are you okay?"

No. She puffed out a breath. "I will be. Once Chastiser is caught. I want to know why he has targeted me. What did I ever do to him?"

"Unfortunately, you may never know. With serial killers, there isn't usually a personal connection. It's more about what characteristics or commonality the victims have. Like his other victims, you were a teenage runaway. You used drugs and were—"

"I know all that," she interrupted him. There was no need for him to point out all her flaws and past mistakes. "But I was already off the streets when he attempted to kill me. I was clean…five months sober. I worked a job and was saving money so I could eventually go to night school."

"Five months sober? But you'd only been at your job three weeks. Where did you live prior to landing the job at the truck stop. I'm guessing, if you were sober, you had escaped the people pushing you to do drugs and trafficking you."

Clasping her hands in her lap, she stared out the front window. Even though she always shared her story with the women she counseled, as motivation that they, too, could have a better life, talking about it with Landon made her feel like anything but a success story. Instead of feeling proud of how far she'd come, she felt ashamed of where she'd been and what she'd done.

"I only asked because I'm wondering if you crossed paths with Chastiser during the time you were working on getting sober," Landon said softly.

She released a shaky breath. "When I realized, if I didn't escape the situation I was in, I would likely be dead before I made it out of my teens, I called a help hotline. The number was posted on the information board at the convenience store. The person on the other end of the phone helped me get into a two-week rehab program. After that, I moved into a temporary residence for recovering addicts trying to get back on their feet."

Brooklyn turned to face Landon. "Unless Chastiser is a reformed addict or the middle age house mom who ran the temporary shelter, I doubt I crossed paths with him during that time."

They rode in silence as Landon circled through a neighboring subdivision before turning back in the direction they'd come.

"Get my phone and text Agent Knight that there's been another attack. I have his number saved in my contacts."

She pulled his phone out of the cup holder where he'd placed it and quickly did as he instructed. There was an immediate reply. "He'll meet us at your house in ten minutes."

She had just replaced the phone when it rang, and Heath Dalton's name flashed on the car sound system display. Landon pressed a button on the steering wheel. "Hello, Heath."

"Are you and Brooklyn safe?"

"For the moment." Landon activated his blinker and turned on to the street where he lived. "News sure travels fast."

"Jackson Knight texted me. I asked him to keep me in the loop if anything happened."

Blue lights strobed up ahead. One police vehicle was parked at the curb and the other was parked in the drive.

"If you need a place to stay," Heath continued, "I co-own a hunting cabin with my brother-in-law. It's near Knotty Pines. You're welcome to stay there until Chastiser is captured, or at least until we can move Brooklyn to a safe house."

Her breath caught. Would she have to go into protective custody? If she refused, how many of her friends and acquaintances would Chastiser go after?

"Thanks. I'll let you know if we need it. We'll stay at a motel tonight and consider our other options tomorrow." Landon disconnected the call and pulled into the driveway, parking beside the police vehicle. "Stay here while I check everything out."

"What if the shooter comes back?" Brooklyn asked, praying Landon couldn't hear the fear in her voice.

"He won't try to snatch you with police here. It would be too risky. Keep the doors locked, and don't get out of the vehicle."

He slipped his Glock into his waistband and exited the vehicle, leaving the keys in the ignition. She clicked the lock button on the door and rubbed her hands over her arms to ward off an anxiety-induced chill.

Dear Lord, what am I going to do? I can't put others' lives in danger. As long as I'm in the picture, Landon and all our employees will be targets. But I'm terrified of being alone. Even with two officers and Landon in plain view, sitting alone in this vehicle is making my anxiety soar.

Landon crossed to the officers standing in front of the open garage door. "I'm Landon Wentworth, the home-owner."

"Are you the one who reported the incident?" the tallest officer asked.

"Yes. Actually, my business partner—" Landon pointed at Brooklyn, sitting in his car watching the discussion "—phoned it in. We were both in the home during the attack."

"We've checked the perimeter. There were no signs of anyone lurking about. Do you want us to check inside?"

"I imagine he took off after we left." He looked toward his vehicle once more. "But we can't take any chances. If one of you will stay with Ms. Thomas, I'll go inside with the other one to make sure the shooter isn't hiding anywhere."

"Sir, it's best for civilians to stay out of the way and let us do our jobs," the older officer said.

Landon leaned in and read the name tag. "I understand, Officer Henderson, but I *am* a trained law enforcement officer. I worked for the Federal Bureau of Investigation for twelve years and currently work as a private investigator. Please, if you would so kindly allow, I'd like to accompany you into *my* home. However, we have good reason to believe Ms. Thomas is the primary target, so it's imperative someone guard her."

"This is highly unusual." Henderson turned to the taller officer. "Grayson, stay with Ms. Thomas. I'll clear the house with Mr. Wentworth."

In his rush to get Brooklyn as far away from Chastiser as he could, Landon had failed to close the garage door, leaving his home vulnerable. He slipped his weapon out of his waistband and nodded for Officer Henderson to follow him. Then he led the way through the garage and into his home. After completing a thorough check of every room on both floors, they returned to the kitchen, where the acidic smell of the smoke bombs still lingered.

"There wasn't anything out of place during our search. Do you think this could be a prank by a kid?"

"Do I think a juvenile threw smoke bombs into my home then shot at my vehicle as I left?" Landon fought to keep the sarcasm out of his voice. "No. I do not. This was not a prank. It was an orchestrated attack on me and Ms. Thomas. The FBI is investigating a recent assault on Ms. Thomas at her home two nights ago. Actually, Agent Jackson Knight should arrive any minute."

"Did I hear my name?" Agent Knight asked, coming through the door from the garage leading into the kitchen.

Landon quickly made the introductions. "Thank you for getting here so fast."

Agent Knight looked around. "No signs of Chastiser in the house?"

"No. Not—"

"Did you say *Chastiser*? As in the serial killer?" Officer Henderson asked.

"Yes," Agent Knight replied. "We believe he's the person responsible for setting fire to Ms. Thomas's house, so it's safe to assume he'd be the one behind the attack tonight."

"What can I do to help?" Officer Henderson stood up straighter and squared his shoulders, awe on his face.

It was a look Landon had seen several times on agents' faces when he worked for the bureau. Not to say that all suspects and crimes weren't important, but there were certain cases that most law enforcement officers craved to be involved in so they could, hopefully, be the one to arrest the elusive criminal.

"Actually, it would be a tremendous help if you could arrange regularly scheduled patrols in the area to monitor this property until we capture Chastiser." Officer Henderson's shoulders slumped, and Agent Knight rushed on. "He may or may not come back here. If he does, it's imperative that we know immediately."

"Yes, sir. I'll arrange for officers to patrol the area every couple of hours." The officer turned to Landon. "Since Agent Knight is here, Officer Grayson and I will be on our way."

"Thank you for responding so quickly, Officer Henderson." Landon opened the door and motioned for the officer to lead the way outside.

Standing with Agent Knight in the shadows of the garage, he watched as the officers climbed into their vehicles and left. "We can't stay here. You smelled the smoke. Even if I thought it was safe, it wouldn't be good for Brooklyn, especially since she's still healing from inhaling smoke during the fire at her house."

Agent Knight turned to him. "I agree. Do you have another place you can stay tonight?" He studied Landon. "I can move Ms. Thomas to a safe house tomorrow, but it will take me a few hours to arrange everything."

"I'd prefer not to be put in a safe house—guarded by strangers—if possible." Brooklyn spoke, coming up beside them.

Landon turned to her. "I thought I asked you to stay in the car."

"When the officers left, I took it as an all-clear sign."

He tamped down his annoyance at her flippant refusal to follow instructions. However, he couldn't blame her for wanting to be part of the conversation. If he were in her position, he'd insist on being included, too. "Fair enough. But, please, step inside the garage, out of sight."

Agent Knight stepped back, and she slipped past him to stand beside Landon's Jeep, which sat in the second garage bay, the closed door blocking her from view.

"So, what's the plan? And do I get any say in the matter?" She crossed her arms over her chest and leaned against the Jeep.

"Ms. Thomas—"

"Brooklyn." A small smile lifted one corner of her lips. "I have a feeling the three of us will have several interactions before you capture Chastiser, so let's skip the formalities. I'm Brooklyn." She jerked her head toward him. "He's Landon, and you're Jackson."

"Okay. Brooklyn," Jackson replied. "I can't force you

to accept our protection, but I will advise you to take this matter seriously. Your life is in danger."

"I know that. Probably better than either of you... And I have the scars to prove it. Which is why I have to have some control over the situation. I'm sure your agents are highly trained at keeping people alive, but I need to be with someone I know—someone I can trust." She pinned Landon with her gaze, a pleading look in her eyes. "I need to stay with Landon."

"Good. We're on the same page. Because I don't intend to let you out of my sight."

A lump formed in his throat, and he forced himself to swallow. Brooklyn was the most independent person he'd ever met. She was a leader who took charge of every situation without fear, as she had done now, letting Jackson know he couldn't intimidate her. That she was turning to Landon for support, acknowledging that she needed *him*, was so out of character for her it was almost enough to bring him to his knees.

Please, Lord, don't let me fail her.

Brooklyn watched as Landon and Jackson exchanged a look. She had to speak up if she wanted a say in what happened next. And honestly, the only person's judgment she trusted was hers. Well, and Landon's. But only when he wasn't trying to coddle her.

"Sheriff Dalton offered us the use of his cabin. I'm sure he wouldn't have suggested it unless he thought it was a good option." She'd never enjoyed relying on others for help, but in this case, if it meant avoiding a safe house where she'd be confined to a small area, she'd happily take up the sheriff on his offer.

Two sets of eyes turned in her direction. Jackson

scratched his head, and a muscle near Landon's temple twitched—something that often happened when he was in deep thought.

"We'll stay in a motel tonight," Landon said after a long pause. "There's a small out-of-the-way place in Townsend where there won't be as many prying eyes."

"And you'll be safe there?" Jackson inquired.

He sighed. "Hopefully. You talk to Heath. Find out everything you can about the cabin. If you think it's a good option, we'll go there. *But* if you think Brooklyn would be more secure in a safe house of your choosing, then that's where we'll go." He turned to her. "*Both of us.* I won't leave you."

Relief swelled inside her, and she was incapable of forming words. She nodded.

"Looks like we have a plan," Jackson declared. "I'll follow you to the motel, keeping my distance so it's not obvious."

"Thanks," Landon replied. "Just give us a few minutes to grab overnight bags, okay?"

"Be quick."

Brooklyn didn't need to be told twice. She power walked across the open span of the garage, pausing as she entered the kitchen to glance back at the men.

"Can you pull the Mustang into the garage while we're packing?" Landon asked Jackson. "The keys are in it."

"Sure thing."

The agent jogged toward the car as Landon followed her into the kitchen. "Why did you ask him to do that?"

"We left in the Mustang because it was faster. But the Jeep will be more practical if we go to Heath's cabin in the mountains." He raised an eyebrow. "You question everything, don't you?"

An involuntary smile sprang to her face. "It was one of the first things Lillian taught me to do."

His laughter spurred her onward as she raced up the stairs. Before Lillian had welcomed Brooklyn into her life, Brooklyn had been too afraid to voice an opinion, having been taught at a young age the dangers of speaking her mind. She had endured many face slaps, punches and name callings, eventually learning to swallow any word that might provoke wrath. One fateful night she'd had enough and she'd voiced her anger, then locked herself in her room before sneaking out the window to meet her boyfriend, Larry, an eighteen-year-old who had promised to always be there for her. Unfortunately, she hadn't realized he'd had ulterior motives until it was too late and she had no place to go.

No. Brooklyn shook her head. *Remember what Lillian said. Reliving the past serves no purpose other than to bring you pain and self-doubt. Learn from it. Forget it. And move on.*

Ten minutes later, she tromped back down the stairs with the old leather backpack Lillian had gifted her on her first day of college on her shoulders. She had located it in the closet and packed it with the items she and Landon had purchased at the store earlier, along with a pair of tennis shoes and an old sweatshirt she'd also found in the closet.

Landon met her at the foot of the stairs, his backpack slung across one shoulder. "Ready?"

She shrugged. "As I'll ever be."

He raised his hand as if he were going to take her bag, then paused and turned toward the door. "Let's not keep Jackson waiting."

Brooklyn followed behind him silently. Had she been too vocal earlier, expressing her desires to be treated as an equal? She didn't want Landon walking on eggshells around her, afraid to speak or offer a helping hand. And while she'd like her opinion to be respected and considered, she also wouldn't complain if he carried her heavy bag. Guess she couldn't have it both ways.

After tossing her bag into the back seat, she climbed into the Jeep and fastened her seat belt. "Why are both of your vehicles black? I know your favorite color is blue."

"Is that right?" He backed the Jeep out of the garage, then hit the button on the visor to lower the garage door. "I didn't realize you knew so much about me."

"It was important to Lillian that you and I got along. She wanted us all to be a happy family. Her opinion was important to me, so I asked her to take me shopping my first Christmas so I could pick out a present for you." Brooklyn smiled at the memory of the tough-as-nails woman who had believed in her more than anyone in her life ever had. "Not knowing what you liked, it seemed safest to buy you a—"

"Blue Henley shirt with long sleeves and three buttons at the neck."

She gasped. "You remember?"

"I do." He glanced in the rearview mirror, activated his blinker and turned right. "It was the softest, most comfortable, perfect-shade-of-cobalt-blue shirt I'd ever owned. I wore it often… Actually, I'm pretty sure I still have it."

She captured her bottom lip between her teeth to quell the smile that threatened. Why did it make her so happy to know he'd appreciated the gift that had taken her hours to select? She had wandered the mall, going from store to store, examining all the blue shirts in the men's department until she'd found what she'd felt was the perfect one. It was nice to know he'd liked it, too. "Okay, so that brings me back to my question. Since you love the color blue, why are both of your vehicles black?"

"Simple. If you don't want your vehicle to stand out, choose white, gray or black. They are ordinary. Almost seventy percent of the vehicles on the road fit into one of those three color categories."

"I always thought guys liked for their vehicles to stand out."

"Most do. If they don't work as private investigators."

"I never thought about it before, but that makes sense." A blanket of silence settled over the vehicle. And she watched the scenery pass by, her mind searching for something to talk about.

"May I ask you something?"

She turned toward him. "Sure."

"I've noticed you often ask random questions—like my preference of vehicle colors. Why?"

"What do you mean? Can't someone simply be inquisitive?"

He glanced at her. Even though his face was in the shadows, she could feel his blue eyes assessing her. He turned his attention back to the road without commenting. Of all the people she'd ever met, Landon was the one person who she'd never been able to hide things from. For some odd reason, she found that comforting. Could it be, in the past year, while they'd been working together to run the agency, they'd become the family Lillian had always hoped for? Hmm. The idea didn't repel her. It might be nice to have an honorary brother to share holidays with when she was an old woman with a house full of pets. Maybe he'd find a nice woman to marry somewhere along the way and have children who would want to visit Auntie Brooklyn and her zoo.

"I think you ask random questions when you're nervous," Landon said in a matter-of-fact tone, interrupting her thoughts. "I've also noticed you doing the same thing when there's a long stretch of silence."

Hugging her middle, she sank deeper into the corner. She wasn't sure how to respond. Landon had the same knack as his aunt for seeing past the invisible shield Brooklyn tried to keep in place. Even if she knew how to explain her need for constant dialogue, she wasn't sure he'd understand. The first year after her stepdad had died, their neighbor, Mrs. Fischer, had let Brooklyn hang out at her house with her three young children while Brooklyn's mom worked. Then Mr. Fischer's job was transferred and the family moved to Miami. After that, she'd been on her own. Most days she hadn't even seen her mom, who would leave for work before Brooklyn got up and would stumble home well into the night after Brooklyn had cried herself to sleep. She would never understand how her mom had held down a job for as long as she had, drinking so heavily and only getting a few hours' sleep each night. Sometimes she wondered if her mom had ceased trying to live a somewhat normal life after Brooklyn had been taken away. Had she stopped going to work and stayed home drinking day and night? Was that what sent her to an early grave?

"I'm sorry." Landon spoke softly.

"For what?" She pulled her arms tighter around her waist.

"I shouldn't have asked you to explain yourself. It's good to be inquisitive. Aunt Lillian always told me if I wanted to know something to ask." He turned into the Shady Mountain Motel, parked under the awning at the front, turned the engine off and put the Jeep into Park. "I bet you and Lillian had some of the best conversations. She loved people who asked questions."

Brooklyn smiled, recalling the heated discussions she and Lillian had participated in, debating everything from ice cream flavors to politics. Tears stung her eyes and her throat tightened. Oh, how she missed her mentor. If only she could talk to her one more time, to hear Lillian tell her everything would be okay. Of all the people Brooklyn had lost in her lifetime, Lillian had hurt the most.

You don't need me. You're going to be just fine on your own. The words of advice Lillian had imparted when Brooklyn left for graduate school echoed from the recesses of Brooklyn's memory. *Remember, you don't have to keep your guard up all the time. It's okay to let people in. Go to church. You will meet nice, like-minded people there. Call me once a week. And talk to God daily. Thank Him for your blessings.*

"Thank You, Lord, for Landon, my protector," she whispered.

"What was that?" Landon asked, opening his door.

She reached for her door handle. "I'm coming. You're not leaving me here alone."

Exiting the vehicle, she rushed to his side. It had taken her and Lillian a while to understand each other, but once they did, they had become the best of friends. Maybe, if she heeded her former mentor's advice and let down her guard, she and Landon could become just as good friends as she and Lillian had been.

FIVE

Landon held the door open for Brooklyn, following her into a room with two double beds. He wasn't thrilled their rooms were on the second story of the two-story motel, but it had been the only way to have adjoining rooms. Even though it was the middle of the week, during the offseason, the front desk clerk had told them the hotel was booked to ninety percent capacity. At least the motel had been designed so that the rooms opened to the outside. Landon breathed a sigh of relief that their rooms were only two doors away from the stairs leading to the ground level, which helped him feel less confined.

Closing the door behind them, he locked the dead bolt, then closed the curtains over the large picture window. Crossing to the adjoining door, he entered the second room and repeated the security steps.

"All good?" Brooklyn asked from behind him.

He turned and offered her what he hoped was a reassuring smile. "I think so. Do you have a preference concerning the rooms?"

She looked from one room to the next. "They're mirror images of each other."

Landon chuckled. "Yeah. Tell you what, you take this room. If anyone was watching us enter, they would assume we're sharing that room—that is, if they didn't see me closing the curtains in this one."

"That sounds logical." She crossed to the bed farthest from the door, dropped her backpack onto it and turned to face him. "Thank you for getting two rooms."

"You're welcome. The only thing I ask is that you leave the adjoining door open."

"Of course." She unzipped her backpack and pulled out shorts and a T-shirt, her Bible, and a small clear bag with a toothbrush and toothpaste inside it. Then she met his gaze. "If you don't mind, I'm going to get ready for bed. It's past midnight and…"

"Oh. Of course." He backed toward the open door that led to his room. "If you need anything…or get frightened… just yell. I'm a light sleeper, so…"

Brooklyn offered a closed-lip smile. "Thanks. I'm sure I'll be fine. It's just for one night, right?"

Nodding, he stepped into his own room. *That was awkward.* He scrubbed a hand over his face. *How could I have been so dense? Just standing around, as she was hinting it was time for me to vacate her room.*

The sound of running water came from next door. Even though Landon doubted Chastiser would find them here, he wouldn't be able to fall asleep until he knew Brooklyn was settled in for the night. Ten minutes later, he heard the bathroom door open, and he listened as she moved around her room. Before long, the light went out and the mattress creaked as she climbed into bed.

"Good night, Landon," she said in a manner reminiscent of an old television series where all the family members would say good-night at the end of the show.

He smiled. "Good night, Brooklyn. Sweet dreams."

Now, why had he said that? He had never, in all his

thirty-six years, told anyone to have *sweet dreams*. He kicked off his shoes and settled back on the bed closest to the door—lying on top of the covers, his arms folded under his head—and stared up at the ceiling.

Lord, please let us be safe here for the night, and let Brooklyn get the rest she needs for her body to heal from the smoke she inhaled. Please, let Agent Knight capture the killer soon.

He pulled out his phone to check for a message from Jackson or Heath. Nothing. Relying on others to make decisions frustrated him. There were few things he hated more than being in limbo. Should he text them? He hadn't asked Heath where the cabin was. What if it was in a location where Landon didn't feel like he could protect Brooklyn? *The sheriff wouldn't send you some place he felt was unsafe. He, of all people, understands the need to protect a woman in danger.*

Heath and his wife Kayla's encounter with killers on a hiking trail inside the Great Smoky Mountains National Park sixteen months ago had been all over the news. Everything might have worked out in the end—with the two of them finding love and happiness—but it easily could have ended in tragedy, especially when one of the killers abducted Kayla and held her hostage. One misstep and, instead of a wedding, it would have ended with a funeral for one or both of them.

While Landon knew wedding bells would never be in his future, he'd like a happy ending for Brooklyn—one that ended with him and Brooklyn surviving the attacks from Chastiser and continuing their work with the foundation, building on the legacy Aunt Lillian had left behind. And maybe one day Brooklyn could find her prince charming and have the life she should have had growing up. A home full of love with a husband and a house full of children who would know Landon as their fun uncle. The thought put a smile on his face.

Some time later, the blaring sound of a smoke alarm jolted him awake. He jumped out of bed, slid his gun off the nightstand and tucked it in his waistband, then rushed toward Brooklyn's room, bumping into her in the connecting doorway.

"What's going on? Did Chastiser find us?" she yelled above the noise, her hands over her ears.

He didn't believe in coincidences and suspected neither did she. "I don't know, but I don't like it. Grab your backpack and let's get out of here."

The sounds of people exiting their rooms and running along the concrete walkway mingled with the sound of the alarm. She quickly did as he asked, returning with her backpack on her shoulders. He snagged his pack off the chair in the corner close to the window and looped it over one shoulder, then pulled back the curtain to see the commotion. A group of guys who looked like they might be part of a construction crew were making their way toward the stairs. Maybe he and Brooklyn could step outside when the group got even with their room door and blend in with them, making their way to his vehicle.

Brooklyn peered over his shoulder. He turned and met her gaze. Landon could only imagine the fear coursing through her at the thought that Chastiser was behind the alarm. "See the group of people headed this way? We're going to exit with them, using them as a wall of protection against prying eyes."

She nodded. He moved to the door and inched it open, aware of her holding on to the back of his shirt. The men drew even. Landon pulled the door open, reached back and clasped her hand then pushed his way out onto the concrete walkway that ran the length of the building, keeping a tight hold on Brooklyn. They were shoved and jostled as the other occupants made their way to the stairs.

The smell of smoke filled the air. Okay, the fire was real. As he questioned what had caused it, the hairs at the nape of his neck stood at attention. He slipped his hand up Brooklyn's arm and wrapped his arm around her shoulder, hugging her to his side. They made their way to the stairs and started down.

"The instant we hit the sidewalk, I'll unlock the Jeep. We need to get out of here. Fast."

Her head jerked in his direction, her eyes round as saucers. Someone bumped into them from behind. She stumbled. He tightened his grip, keeping her upright. After taking two more steps, they were on the sidewalk, racing to his Jeep. Landon hit the unlock button on his key fob. The lights flashed, followed by a clicking sound. They tossed their packs into the back, then settled into their respective seats. Brooklyn clicked her seat belt into place as he pressed the start button, then shifted into Reverse. He caught sight of smoke and flames coming from the back of the building.

"Don't forget your seat belt," Brooklyn commanded.

Landon put the Jeep into Drive, maneuvered around a group of people standing in the parking lot and headed for the exit, pulling onto the main highway as a fire truck pulled into the entrance. He reached for his seat belt with one hand and looped it over him. Brooklyn leaned over, taking the buckle and latching it into place.

"Thank you." He tightened his grip on the steering wheel.

"You're welcome." She settled back into her seat. "Where are we headed?"

A dark-colored truck sped out of the motel parking lot, racing after them. Its bumper inches behind the Jeep's.

"I don't know, but the first thing we have to do is lose the vehicle following us."

Brooklyn twisted in her seat and looked out the back window. The windows on the other vehicle were tinted, making it impossible to ID the other driver even when they drove under a streetlight.

"I need you to turn around and brace yourself. We may be in for a bumpy ride."

She did as he instructed, pulling her seat belt taut over her shoulder and midsection. "What's the plan? Do you want me to call nine-one-one?"

He shook his head. "No. Townsend is a small town with an equally small police force. The on-duty officer will be at the motel assisting with the fire. I'd hate to pull them away from the scene of a crime that could affect innocent people."

"*We're* innocent people, too. We didn't ask to be put in this situation. Don't we count?" Brooklyn didn't mean to sound selfish, but she wanted someone to stop the killer coming after her. She puffed out a breath and blew a strand of her hair out of her eyes.

"Of course we count. And we'll call Heath for help as soon as we lose the vehicle tailing us." He spared a quick glance in her direction. "I'll keep you safe. Trust me."

I'll keep you safe. Trust me. His words echoed the ones his aunt had said to her when she'd pulled Brooklyn out of the burning coffin fifteen years ago. Lillian was the first person Brooklyn had ever trusted, but the instant she'd looked into the older woman's blue eyes, she'd known Lillian would do whatever she said she would. She saw the same truth in Landon's eyes.

"I do." Now, why had she chosen those words to affirm her trust in him? In the close quarters they found themselves in at the moment, the words had sounded more intimate than she'd intended. S*top. You're overthinking, as usual. Landon thought nothing of your word choice. And neither should you.* "May I ask what your plan is?"

"My plan is to lose him, then get to Heath's cabin." He pulled his Glock out of his waistband and handed it to her.

"What do you want me to do with this?"

"Hold it or put it in the glove compartment. It was pinching my side. But I need it close, just in case…" He sped up.

She put the weapon in the glove compartment and watched in the side mirror as the vehicle following them mimicked Landon's moves. "He's still there."

"I know. Hang on." He took a sharp left, his Jeep leaning ever so slightly as the two tires on her side lifted off the ground.

She clutched the dashboard. *Please, Lord, don't let us wreck.*

He drove out of the turn and the tires bounced back onto the road, regaining traction. Landon floored the gas pedal and sped along the curvy mountain road at a speed that dizzied her mind. If it wasn't the early morning hours when most people were still sleeping, she'd be worried about meeting other vehicles in the curves.

"Do you know where you're going?"

"Yes. I used to drive these roads when I was a teenager. One of my best friends lived out here. There's a hidden drive up ahead. If I can reach it well before him, we can pull in and wait for him to pass us. There are tall trees blocking the drive from view."

"How much farther?"

"Another mile or so. There is a series of three switchback

curves before the road straightens. The drive is immediately after the last curve, at the beginning of the straightaway." He sped up as he spoke, and she watched as the other vehicle fell back several car lengths. *Please, Lord, let Landon's plan work.*

Her right hand clutched the grab bar. She held her breath as he took a curve at sixty miles per hour. He was trying to get them to safety, but she wanted to be alive when they got there.

The vehicle behind them fell farther back. Once they cleared the second curve, the vehicle was out of sight. But she wouldn't breathe a sigh of relief until they had lost Chastiser.

The third switchback came into view. Landon zoomed into it, then slowed as he entered the curve. The road straightened.

"Where's the drive? I don't see it?" She didn't attempt to hide the panic in her voice.

The Jeep came even with a large oak tree. Landon jerked the steering wheel to the right and drove into a thicket of shrubs, trees and underbrush. Limbs beat at the top and sides of the vehicle as the tires bounced over the rough terrain. Brooklyn was thankful the hardtop was in place to protect them.

He slammed to a stop in front of a small, dilapidated house, shifted into Park, cut the engine and turned off all lights. They both twisted in their seats and stared out the back window, silence blanketing the vehicle. Brooklyn held her breath. After a minute or two, the truck zoomed past their hiding spot.

She met Landon's gaze. "Let's go chase him! We can get the jump on him and—"

"Not on your life," he declared, opening his door and getting out.

"Why not? We could catch him."

"Because you're with me. And I won't put your life in danger like that." He closed the door and walked toward the road.

Jumping out of the Jeep, she fought her way through the underbrush and met him at the back of the vehicle. "What are you doing?"

"Getting a better view of the road so I can see when he's out of sight."

She followed him to the edge of the road and watched as the car's taillights got smaller and smaller. This stretch of road was flat and straight, providing a driver with a clear view of what was ahead and behind them. Several minutes later, the vehicle drove out of sight.

"Okay, let's go." Landon cupped her elbow and guided her back to the Jeep.

They backed out of the hidden drive as the first orange, red and yellow strokes of sunrise painted the sky. If she weren't on the run to save her life, she would have wanted to pause to appreciate the beauty of God's artwork. *Lord, Your artistic masterpieces have no rivals. Thank You for the reminder that every day is a new and beautiful beginning. Please protect Landon as he strives to keep me alive. Lord, I pray Chastiser is captured and punished for his crimes. His victims deserve justice.*

Fifteen years ago, before Lillian came into her life, Brooklyn had considered herself an agnostic. She had never seen evidence of God's existence, but she hadn't been certain He didn't exist, either. However, she had believed, if He existed, He had forgotten about her and didn't care what happened to her. Then Lillian rescued her.

After Brooklyn moved in with her, she slowly planted the seeds of salvation in Brooklyn's mind. Even more than the fact that Lillian had saved her from Chastiser, Brooklyn would forever be thankful Lillian had taught her God's word and the steps to becoming a Christian. Whatever this life threw her way, she had God's love and the hope of Heaven to get her through.

But that did not mean that she would sit back and wait for Chastiser to kill her. She would not go down without a fight. Brooklyn had the support of the man beside her. He was willing to put his life on the line to help protect hers, and she was appreciative of him. She bowed her head and peered through her eyelashes at Landon. How had she missed his handsome features? Chiseled, square jaw. blue eyes. Wavy brown hair and muscular shoulders. Add in his confidence and protective nature and he was the living, breathing image of one of the cartoon princes she had dreamed of rescuing her and whisking her away to a castle when she was a naive eight-year-old who had thought happily-ever-after existed. But then she had grown up—fast!

SIX

Brooklyn climbed out of the Jeep and stretched. The drive to Heath's hunting cabin had only taken two hours, but her muscles ached as if she'd been sitting for much longer. Of course, part of her fatigue was from being awakened before dawn for the second time in three days. She took in her surroundings. The log cabin sat in a small clearing at the end of a nondescript dirt road on the back side of a thirty-acre tract of land. Even though she couldn't see the water, she could hear the rapids in the river Heath had said ran along the edge of the property. He'd also told them there was a canoe stored in the old shed behind the cabin they were welcome to use. After the events of the past few days, Brooklyn doubted she'd reach the point where she felt safe enough to venture far from the cabin, but she had kept those thoughts to herself. No one needed to know how deeply her fear ran through her veins.

Landon rounded the back of the Jeep, both backpacks in his hands. "Ready to check out the inside?"

"Here, let me take my bag." She reached for the pack, but he dodged her outstretched hand and went around her. "I've got it."

"Well then, open the back, and I'll get the grocery bags."

"They can wait for a few minutes." He held up his hand

and shook the key Heath had given them when they'd showed up at his house just after seven this morning. "Come on. Let's see if the inside of the cabin looks better than the outside."

Landon jogged toward the front door, and she followed close behind.

"I don't know. I think it looks rather nice." She took in the weathered logs and the faded red tin roof before they bound up the steps to the small porch. "I've slept in much worse places. As long as there aren't any spiders inside, I'll be happy here."

Inserting the key into the lock, he paused and turned to her, a quizzical expression on his face. What had she said that warranted such a look? Her fear of spiders? No. Most people had an aversion to creepy-crawly things. *I've slept in much worse places.* That had to be it. She knew Lillian had shared some of the aspects of her childhood with Landon, but she must not have shared all of the nitty-gritty details with him. If she had, he would have known about the month she'd spent sleeping in an abandoned warehouse that had been infested with roaches and rats. Brooklyn wasn't surprised by the omission of facts. After all, Lillian hadn't told her much about Landon's past, either. The only way Brooklyn had found out about Landon's tragic childhood had been through an internet search when curiosity about why his aunt had raised him had gotten the better of her. She had told no one what she'd discovered, not even Lillian. Her actions had been an invasion of his privacy. Besides, she figured he wouldn't want to discuss his past any more than she wanted to discuss hers.

"Hurry." She forced a smile, praying he'd let her previous comment pass. "Let's get inside and see what we've gotten ourselves into."

He gave her a curt nod and unlocked the door. Pushing it open, he stepped back to let her enter first. She walked across the threshold and took in the open living, dining and kitchen space. The cabin was comfortably furnished. The dining area, had a table with four chairs, and in the living room, a leather sofa and a recliner offered ample seating. To the right of the living room, there was a set of stairs leading to a balcony above.

"Heath said there are two bedrooms and one bathroom." Landon tossed the backpacks onto the sofa. "One bedroom is upstairs, and the other is down." He pointed toward the hall off the dining area. "If you don't mind, I'll take the first-floor bedroom so if someone breaks in, I'll be between them and you."

"That's fine."

Last week, before Chastiser had shown back up in her life, she would have declared that she didn't need protecting and would have insisted on taking the first-floor bedroom to prove her independence. However, at the moment, she didn't have the energy to pretend a bravery she didn't feel. The events of the past few days had shattered her naive confidence that she could survive anything life threw her way.

Without another word, she grabbed her backpack and took off up the stairs to explore. As she reached the landing at the top of the stairs, she heard Landon opening and closing doors downstairs, probably checking out his own bedroom and the bathroom.

The upstairs bedroom turned out to be an open loft. The bed was positioned far enough back from the railing that it couldn't be seen from the first floor. There was an old oak dresser with a mirror, a nightstand and a small wardrobe. Someone had decorated the space in a bright yellow and blue floral pattern. Most likely, Heath's wife. Brooklyn had first met Kayla—a nurse practitioner—a year ago, a few months after the other woman had moved to Barton Creek. Brooklyn had cut her hand on a piece of broken glass and had gone to the clinic for stitches. Kayla was a competent, down-to-earth person. Living in a small town, they ran into each other regularly and eventually had become friends.

"Brooklyn," Landon yelled from below. "I'm going to bring in the groceries."

She dropped her backpack onto the bed and crossed to the railing, looking down in time to see him opening the front door. "I'll help."

"No need. I can get all the bags in one trip. But I won't complain if you want to help me cook. It's way past breakfast time." He disappeared out the door, whistling a tune as he went.

Why is he so happy? Brooklyn headed downstairs, recalling how he used to whistle as he'd do chores—mowing and minor repairs—around his aunt's house when he'd come home between semesters. When she'd asked Lillian about it, the older woman had said some people were happiest with busy hands. Landon was one of those people. The busier he was, the happier he was. However, she couldn't recall a single time in the past year when she'd heard him whistle. And it had been a busy year for the foundation. Surely he couldn't be happy to be on the run with her? Who in their right mind would want to be stuck in a cabin in the middle of the woods while a serial killer looked for them?

She went into the small kitchen area and started opening cabinets. The kitchen was well stocked with canned food, dinnerware, pots and pans, and cast-iron skillets. There was also a built-in air fryer/microwave combo. Brooklyn had no clue what a typical hunting cabin looked like, but the furnishings and supplies in Heath's cabin far exceeded her expectations.

Landon came inside, his arms laden with bags. "Easy-peasy."

He shuffled to the dining area and placed the bags on the table. Then he flexed a muscle, and she laughed. He seemed to be in a playful mood. She wasn't sure what brought it on, but she would not be the one to squash his joy. After all, with Chastiser after them, any happy moments would be short-lived.

"That was delicious." Landon pushed his chair back from the table, picked up both his and her plates, and carried them to the sink. Plugging the basin, he turned on the hot water and added a small amount of liquid detergent.

"You don't have to do that. I can wash up," Brooklyn said from his side.

"Not a chance." He smiled. "You made the omelets— and your cooking skills are much better than mine, so I hope you will continue to be the chef. I will do my part by being the dishwasher."

Landon picked up a handful of suds, turned and blew them at her. She giggled, her face lighting up. Then she dipped her finger into the sink and put a dollop of suds on his nose the same way Aunt Lillian used to do when he would sulk about doing chores in the kitchen. He much preferred working outside. But if he could continue to put a smile on her face, he would happily do all the chores. Laughing, he picked up a dish towel and wiped his face.

He had tried several times since they had arrived at the cabin to get her to smile—whistling, flexing a muscle after he carried in the groceries, telling jokes while she cooked.

If he'd known all it would take was a few soapsuds, he would have started with that.

"This won't take long." He removed his watch, pulled a dishcloth out of the drawer and plunged his hands into the water. After running the cloth over a dirty plate, he set the dish in the adjoining sink.

Brooklyn shifted the faucet, turned it on and rinsed the dish. Then she placed it in the drying rack.

He nodded at the dish towel. "I'll wash and rinse. You dry."

"Okay."

She picked up the towel, dried the plate and placed it on the counter. They worked in silence and soon all the dishes had been washed, dried and put away. Growing up an only child, Landon had never had anyone to share chores with. Surprisingly, doing dishes with Brooklyn was enjoyable, and it didn't hurt that her help had reduced the time the chore would have taken.

"That's it. All done." She folded the dish towel and placed it on the counter by the empty drying rack.

"Thank you for your help." He looked around the cabin.

Now what? If they were at his house, they would probably each go to their respective offices and complete paperwork. It felt strange not having anything to do. He spotted a television in the built-in entertainment center along with two shelves of DVDs.

"Do you—"

"I think—"

They spoke in unison.

He smiled. "You go first."

"I was just going to say that I thought I'd head upstairs."

"Oh." Why did that disappoint him? They'd never been the type of people to hang out together. Even during the times he had come home on college breaks, they had each done their own things. He regretted that now. There was no way of knowing how long they'd have to hide out here. If they couldn't learn to be in the same room together, the situation would become even more awkward.

"What were you going to say?" she inquired.

"I was going to suggest we look through the DVDs to see if we could find a movie to watch."

She turned to look across the room at the collection of movies, her mouth forming an O.

"It's okay. I'm sure you're tired. You may want to take a nap. After all, we were up before dawn."

She glanced at the stairs, then turned back to him a smile on her face that didn't quite reach her eyes, and he knew he'd correctly guessed her reason for wanting to go to her room. "A movie. Why not?" She walked to the bookcase and started skimming the shelves. "I don't remember the last time I watched a movie. There never seems to be enough time for leisure activities."

"I'm sure you would prefer the nap." He wished he hadn't mentioned the movie now.

"No, not at all." She looked up at him, one eyebrow raised. "I'm just wondering if you and I can agree on a genre. What types of movies do you prefer?"

What should he say? He wanted her to enjoy the movie, but he wasn't into watching romantic comedies. Landon didn't see her as a science fiction fan and, considering their current situation, could not imagine she'd want to watch a suspense. He moved closer and examined the vast selection of titles. "I'm not hard to please. Whatever you want to watch is fine with me."

"Is that so... Hmm..." She ran a finger along the titles

and pulled a case off the shelf. "How about this one? Do you think you'd enjoy it?"

He recognized the title of a film that released three years prior. It definitely was a movie he wouldn't have chosen. Oh well, sacrificing his dignity was a small price to pay to help take Brooklyn's mind off her worries. "That looks like a…fine choice."

He reached for the movie, and she pulled it back, laughing.

"You have got to be kidding me. There's no way I would watch this. I prefer a movie with substance. Something with an actual plot line where the outcome isn't predictable by the title." She slid the movie back into its place and grabbed a suspense movie. "This is more to my liking."

She crossed to the television, opened the case, paused and looked up. "Unless you think this movie may be too scary?"

He laughed. "You were testing me, weren't you?"

"Yeah, kind of." She giggled, turned on the TV and slid the DVD into the device. Then she settled on the couch. "Your aunt once mentioned that you like to watch scary movies based on real crimes. She said it was probably her fault because she let you watch true crime documentaries with her when you were young."

He dropped onto the couch beside her. Landon smiled as he remembered all the things his aunt had done that the parenting magazines would say were a mistake. If he said so himself, he hadn't turned out half-bad, despite the trauma he'd experienced before coming to live with her. And that was because of the love that she'd heaped upon him.

"I had been living with her for about three months when I woke up in the middle of the night and found her watching a documentary on a cold case. She let me crawl into bed with her and watch it. My parents had never even let me watch the nightly news—trying to shelter me as long as they could. Until the day my dad snapped." Maybe the trauma of his dad killing his mother before committing suicide was why he had such compassion for Brooklyn and what she was going through. Landon's life easily could have been cut short all those years ago. He would never know why his dad had spared his life that day, but he was thankful to be alive and, he hoped, making a difference in the lives of others.

"Lillian never spoke about your parents other than to say your mom was her sister and that there was a large age gap between the two of them. I know your parents died in a tragic accident." She frowned. "I never told Lillian, but... I let my curiosity get the better of me and did an internet search of their names. I'm sorry I invaded your privacy. But most of all, I'm sorry for what you went through."

The faces of all the people who had stood in the funeral line to offer their condolences to him and Lillian flashed through his mind. He recalled how their words had seemed empty. Although he was sure they were sincere, to his seven-year-old ears the words had sounded scripted. It hadn't helped that he'd overhead a few people whispering about him being an orphan. They had feared the circumstances of his parents' deaths would affect him negatively and he would end up being a troubled adult.

Brooklyn's *I'm sorry* had not sounded forced or fake. Other than Aunt Lillian, he believed this was the first time someone understood his pain.

SEVEN

Brooklyn paced from the bed to the loft railing and back again for the umpteenth time. The lack of internet and phone connection was driving her stir crazy. Heath had warned them that the cell service would be spotty, but they hadn't even gotten one call out in the three days they had been at the cabin. She was desperate to know what was going on with the investigation. Were the FBI any closer to identifying Chastiser?

"You're going to wear a hole in the floor if you don't stop pacing," Landon said loudly from the foot of the stairs. "Come on down. I think I've figured out a way to help both of us burn off some of the stress we're feeling."

"Please, Lord, don't let him suggest *another* movie," she muttered under her breath. They had watched more movies since being at the cabin than she'd watched in the last ten years.

"Did you say something?"

"I'll be right there." Brooklyn released a slow breath. *I'm sorry, Lord. I didn't mean to be negative. I appreciate all that Landon has done to keep me safe while trying to keep my mind occupied so I don't let the stress of the situation weigh me down.*

She plastered a smile on her face and headed down the stairs.

Landon greeted her at the bottom step. "I know you're tired of being cooped up, so I've come up with a solution."

Excitement soared inside her. "Oh, boy. We can't be over forty-five minutes from Knotty Pines. Can we go there? I spent six months in a foster home there when I was—"

"Wait. Hold up." He captured her hand. "I'm sorry. I didn't mean that we were going to drive into town."

"Oh." She frowned, pulled her hand free and went around him. "That's okay. I understand. But I don't feel like a hike today. You can go without me. I'll find a movie to watch."

"I wasn't talking about going on a hike. We've already explored the woods—as far as I'm willing to venture into them, anyway. There isn't much else to see."

Wasn't that the truth? Their second day here, he'd wanted to know what—if anything—was nearby. He'd strapped on his gun, and they had hiked through the woods, using the trees to hide their movements. During the last two days, they had discovered there weren't any other cabins within a mile of them.

He had piqued her interest. If they weren't going hiking or to town, what did he have in mind? "Okay, I'm listening."

He crossed to the kitchen area where the backpack they had used during their hikes sat on the countertop. "I want to get you out in the canoe."

She hated to be the voice of reason, especially since he was trying to make sure she didn't just sit around—or pace—but she had to ask, "Is that wise? Being out in the open?"

"Could you give me more credit than that? I'm not sug-gesting we paddle downriver." Landon scowled at her with a raised eyebrow. "When we watched that old Kevin Bacon movie, you mentioned you'd never been white-water rafting. It got me wondering if you'd be able to make it through the rapids unharmed if canoeing out of here was your only method of escape."

"You have a valid point, but that still doesn't change the fact that we'll be out in the open. At least when we were hiking, we had the trees to hide our movements."

"We'll stay in the area behind the cabin. The trees bordering the river block the view of it from the cabin, unless you're on the second-floor balcony. *And* it's mid-October, which is a bit cold for rafting trips, so we shouldn't encounter any other people on the water. We've not seen or heard anyone out on the river since we've been here. Mainly, I want to teach you how to paddle and safely navigate the rapids. What do you say?"

"You're confident we'll be able to hear if anyone tries to sneak up on us?"

A smile split his face. Landon dug into the backpack and pulled out a small device. "I found this in the closet in my bedroom. It's a baby monitor. According to the box, it has a thousand-foot range, which should be plenty. I've turned the volume all the way up, and I've hidden the camera outside where it offers a clear view of the cabin." He looked at the device and shook his head. "I thought Heath said this was a hunting cabin, but it seems like it's more of a vacation home for the entire family."

"You said he co-owns the property with his wife's brother and sister-in-law. They have a young child. I can't blame the women for wanting to tag along and enjoy this peaceful setting while their husbands hunt." It dawned on her that she'd been too critical about being cooped up here. If she had to hide out somewhere, this wasn't a terrible location. She would be enjoying her time here if it weren't for the serial killer hunting her.

"Okay." She nodded. "Seems like you've thought of everything. Just give me a few minutes to change into something more comfortable."

Brooklyn jogged up the stairs and quickly changed into a pair of loose cargo pants and a long-sleeved T-shirt she had found in the wardrobe, thankful Heath and Kayla had told her to help herself to anything she needed that was in the cabin. After slipping her feet into the sneakers she'd purchased after leaving the hospital, she pulled her hair into a ponytail and secured it with an elastic band and then slathered sunscreen on her face and neck. Crossing to the nightstand, she reached for her cell phone, paused and shook her head. No point taking it, since there wasn't likely to be service and getting wet could damage it. Besides, if something happened and she had cell service, she could use her new watch, which was supposed to be water resistant.

Returning downstairs, she found Landon digging in the small pantry. "What are you looking for?"

"Freezer bags. I thought we'd put our cell phones in one to help keep them dry if we were to capsize."

Her eyes widened. "Capsize! I'm not looking to go swimming."

He turned around and waved a box of freezer bags in the air triumphantly. "Neither am I. The water will be cold this time of year. However, it doesn't hurt to be prepared."

She waved off the plastic zipper bag he held out to her. "I left mine upstairs."

He opened the freezer bag, dropped his phone inside, sealed it and tucked it into the side pocket of his pants. After he returned the box to the pantry, he crossed to the entryway and snagged both of their rain jackets off the hooks by the door. He tossed Brooklyn's to her before shrugging into his own, removed his holstered weapon from the top of the refrigerator—where he kept it during the day so it would be close at hand—and tucked it into the inner pocket.

"You're not putting your gun in a bag like your phone?"

He shook his head. "I need to be able to use it quickly. Getting it wet wouldn't be great, but as long as I can dry it within a reasonable amount of time, the gun won't be damaged."

Slipping the backpack onto his shoulders, he nodded at the two folded towels that rested on the table. "Grab those."

She did as he instructed, then followed him onto the small back deck. At the base of the deck there was a small patio with a grill and picnic table. Just beyond that was a fire pit with Adirondack chairs circling it. Brooklyn could picture a family sitting outside on a cool, starry night toasting marshmallows for s'mores. Sadness pierced her heart. As a young girl, she'd dreamed of growing up and being the mom she would have loved to have had. A mom who made memories with her children, taking them camping and making the gooey chocolate treat. But that had been before she had lived on the streets and realized how dark the world truly was.

Even though she had escaped that life when Lillian rescued her and she'd since become a Christian, she could not bear the thought of a child of her own going through what she had. Besides, God may have forgiven her sins, but she highly doubted any man could overlook her past.

A canoe with two paddles, helmets and life jackets inside it rested at the edge of the water. When had Landon carried everything out of the shed? It must have been while she'd been upstairs feeling sorry for herself for being stuck in the middle of nowhere. Shame welled inside her. While she'd been pouting, Landon had been trying to think of ways to make good use of their time at the cabin.

Shrugging out of the backpack, he placed it into the center of the canoe.

"What's in the backpack besides the baby monitor?"

"Bottled water and a couple of protein bars."

"I thought we were staying close. Do we really need a snack?"

"The protein bars were still in there from our hike yesterday. I just didn't remove them." He pointed at two Adirondack chairs tucked under a shade tree close to the river's edge. "Leave the towels on one of those chairs. Hopefully, we won't need them, but if we do, we'll want them to be dry."

After dropping the towels onto the closest chair, she crossed to the canoe. "What's the plan?" She accepted the life jacket and helmet he held out to her.

Landon shrugged into a larger life jacket, his helmet already on his head. "We'll paddle upstream to the weeping willow tree at the edge of the clearing, then circle and come back, going through those two rapids. Once we clear them, we'll make our way back to the bank." He pushed the bow of the canoe into the water, holding firmly to the back. "You sit in the bow, and I'll sit in the stern."

She eyed the canoe—swaying in the water in spite of his firm hold. Bow meant front, but just how was she supposed to get into the vessel without falling into the water? "Remember this is my first time in a canoe, so don't be afraid to give me detailed instructions. I promise I won't be offended."

Landon smiled. "Climb in here at the back, where I'm holding. Then, once you have your balance, walk along the center of the canoe to the seat in the front."

Nodding, she climbed inside and shuffled along the center of the vessel, her arms outstretched like a tightrope walker. After she settled onto the seat, she turned and watched as he pushed the canoe off the shore into ankle-deep water and eased into the canoe, settling on his own seat at the rear.

He bent, picked up a paddle and handed it to her. "Keep it out of the water until I tell you what to do."

Nodding, she grasped the paddle, turned to face front, and laid the handle across her lap. Landon used his paddle to turn the vessel upstream, staying close to the shoreline.

"As you paddle, insert the blade about three-fourths of the way deep and use slow, flowing movements, rotating from one side to the other. Ready?"

She nodded.

"Starting on the left side. Go!"

Brooklyn sliced the surface of the water with the paddle blade, pulled it back, then upward, and switched to the other side, repeating the process.

"Good. You're doing great."

Within a matter of minutes, they were paddling in rhythm. Surprisingly, the exertion it took to move the canoe through the water wasn't as difficult as she'd anticipated, and the vessel glided through the rapids. Thirty-five minutes later, they had made five loops through the rapids, pausing between circles to check the baby monitor.

"Okay, that's enough," Landon said. "You did great."

They rowed close to the shore. Landon climbed out into the water, which came several inches above his shoes, and pulled the back of the canoe onto the grassy area, then held out his hand to help her disembark.

She stepped out of the canoe and removed her helmet and life jacket.

Landon held out his own helmet and life jacket. "Would you put these on the chair, along with yours? I'll grab them when I take the canoe back to the shed."

Accepting the gear, she crossed to the chairs and dumped everything on the empty one before picking up the towels.

After Landon had pulled the canoe fully onto the bank, she held out a towel to him. "Thank you."

His brow furrowed. "For what?"

"Getting me out of the cabin for more than a hike in the woods." She dried the water splatters off her face and hands, then draped the towel around her neck. "I appreciate everything you're doing to keep me alive. And I hope I haven't seemed ungrateful. It's just…"

"Stressful. Depressing. Scary. Boring."

"All of the above…except boring. You've made sure of that." She met his gaze. "I'm sorry I dragged you into this mess, but since I have to be stranded in the woods with someone, I'm glad it's you. You've kept an upbeat attitude while ensuring I eat regular meals and don't spend all my time alone in my room with my thoughts."

Her face warmed. *Why did I say that?* She had spoken the truth, but it had sounded much more intimate than she'd intended. Although she knew, without a doubt, if she were ever stranded on a deserted island and could have only one thing with her, what she'd want the most would be for Landon to be stranded with her. Not because she had romantic intentions—she'd decided long ago that her childhood had been such a mess she'd never want to be a wife or mother for fear she'd be as bad as her own parents—but because he made her feel less afraid.

Pride swelled inside Landon. Not in the puffed-up manner the preacher always cautioned against. It simply filled his heart with joy to be the one Brooklyn wanted by her side during this time. It gave him a sense of paying it forward. After all, Aunt Lillian had been there for him when he needed her the most. She'd never once complained or acted as if it was a burden to be saddled with a kid. He'd always been grateful for her love and guidance during the worst time of his life. It had been his hope that he could do the same for someone else one day. He just hadn't planned for the *someone else* to be Brooklyn and the *one day* to be now. But it didn't matter. This was the situation they found themselves in. He would not leave her side until Chastiser had been captured and she was safe.

Thunder rumbled in the distance. He searched the sky. Dark clouds were rolling in from the southwest.

"We need to get inside." Landon tossed his towel to her and quickly tied the canoe to a nearby tree. He would have preferred putting the canoe and gear back in the shed where they belonged, but that would have to wait until the storm passed. Grabbing the backpack, he grasped Brooklyn's free hand. "Let's go."

The clouds opened, and big, fat raindrops pelted them. As they raced for the cabin, a bolt of lightning zigzagged in the distance. Brooklyn squealed and ducked as if she could hide from the danger. They needed to get inside now. Landon scooped Brooklyn into his arms and ran.

"I can walk," she protested. "Put me down."

"This is faster." He tightened his hold and didn't put her down until they reached the patio.

Landon headed toward the stairs. He stepped back to allow Brooklyn to go up first, but she wasn't there. "Brooklyn?"

"Under here."

Ducking his head, he looked under the deck and spotted her sitting on a built-in wooden bench with brightly colored cushions. "What are you doing?"

She smiled. "Enjoying the rain."

He sat down beside her. "I thought you were afraid of the storm."

"No. The lightning startled me because I wasn't expecting it. But I love rain." She turned to him with pleading eyes. "Is it okay if we sit out here until it passes?"

He probably should insist they go inside, but this was the first genuine smile he'd seen on her face since she escaped the fire at her home. Besides, he had the baby monitor. "Only if it passes quickly. Otherwise, I'll give you ten minutes."

"Deal." Her smile widened.

He wished he could take away all her stress so she could always be as happy as she was in this moment. Taking off the backpack, he set it on the ground and pulled out the baby monitor. Unfortunately, raindrops had collected on the camera lens, blurring the image. With a silent sigh, he put the monitor away and glanced at Brooklyn. Mesmerized by the rain, she sat with one of her feet tucked underneath her and her arms wrapped around her waist, her damp hair hanging in ringlets down her back. She was beautiful. How had he never seen it before?

She met his gaze, her blue eyes sparkling. "The rain has stopped."

Landon looked around. The rain clouds and thunder had shifted to the northeast. He hadn't even noticed. Standing, he held out his hand, and she slipped hers into it. She beamed up at him. A jolt of awareness zinged through Landon. As a moth drawn to a flame, he lowered his head. She closed her eyes and turned her face upward.

Suddenly, the sound of breaking glass and a loud boom reverberated above them. Landon jerked upright. His heart hammering in his chest. He'd have to examine his actions and the near kiss later. First, he'd have to determine the source of the disturbance that had saved him from a grave mistake. Had lightning struck the cabin? They scrambled out from under the deck. The smell of smoke filled the air.

"Stay here… No." He unzipped his jacket and pulled his weapon out of its holster. "Get back to the canoe, in case it's Chastiser."

She grabbed his arm. Fear had replaced the joy that had been in her eyes moments before. "Come with me."

"I'll follow as fast as I can. Now, go." He gave her a gentle push, and she took off toward the river. Walking backward in the same direction, his eyes stayed on the cabin. Fire billowed out of one of the side windows.

There was a loud pop. A bullet flew past—missing him by mere inches—hitting one of the Adirondack chairs.

"Gunfire! Run!" he yelled to Brooklyn.

She looked over her shoulder, her eyes as round as saucers, and froze in place.

Landon raced toward her, his body half turned, gun raised, ready to return fire. He didn't see anyone. Where was the shooter? He reached Brooklyn. "Run!"

She snapped out of her trance and they raced to the canoe. Another shot rang out. It came from the left side of the cabin. He returned fire.

Brooklyn untied the canoe and pushed it into the water. "Come on!"

He tucked his gun into its holster, held the canoe steady for her to get inside, then climbed in behind her. "Head for the rapids."

She followed his instructions. He looked back and saw a dark figure stumbling down the wet lawn. Picking up his paddle, he helped guide the canoe into the rapids in the middle of the river. The water grabbed the canoe and turned the bow downstream, propelling it forward.

Laying down his paddle, he pulled out his gun, then shot at the shadowy figure. The man darted behind a tree. As long as Landon and Brooklyn were out in the open, they were vulnerable. He tucked the gun back into its holster, picked up his paddle and plunged the blade into the water. They had to make it to the opposite shore and to the safety of the woods. Two more gunshots rang out behind them in rapid succession. He ducked. "Paddle harder!"

Landon's arms ached as he struggled to guide the canoe on a path of escape. *Please Lord, let us make it off the river alive.* Another gunshot sounded, and a bullet pierced the lower left side of the canoe. Water gushed into the bottom. If they didn't make it to shore quickly, they would sink and be at the mercy of the rapids.

"What are we going to do?" Panic punctuated Brooklyn's words.

"Continue to paddle on the left side. We have to turn the boat toward shore."

"It's not working."

There was only one choice now. "We have to abandon the canoe."

Fear registered on her face. She pressed her lips together and nodded.

"I'll lean the canoe so the side almost touches the water. Then I want you to dive out as far as you can so you clear the boat and don't get trapped under it."

Another bullet hit the water near them. Landon leaned all his weight against the right side of the boat. Brooklyn dived and he followed her. The canoe capsized, coming down hard on his legs. His upper body had cleared the vessel, but the canoe had trapped his legs under its weight, wedging them against a large boulder nestled just below the surface of the water.

He pushed against the canoe, desperate to free himself. He needed to find Brooklyn. If she had hit her head on one of the boulders when she dived from the canoe, she could be drowning. He struggled but could not free himself. The weight of the water and the canoe pressed against his lower legs. If he couldn't break free of the boat soon, the bones in his legs were likely to snap. Struggling, he pushed upward, lifting the canoe mere inches.

"Let's try together," Brooklyn said from the bow of the canoe.

She slowly made her way to him, pressing against the canoe as she struggled against the force of the churning water. He swallowed a cry as the boat pressed down on his shins, knowing she couldn't reach him without the aid of the canoe steadying her. Finally, she made it beside him and placed her hands under the rim of the canoe.

"Ready?"

He nodded. "Lift!"

They both pushed upward, and Landon pulled his legs free. Another round of gunfire ensued. A bullet pierced the canoe, passing between him and Brooklyn. Chastiser had become desperate. It seemed he no longer cared how Brooklyn died—by fire or a bullet.

"We have to let the rapids carry us away from the shooter," Landon said hurriedly. "Lay on your back, feet downstream and, above all, try not to fight the current."

Without a word, she gave him a quick hug, let go and followed his instructions. He watched as the waters swirled her body away. Then he followed suit.

The current carried them away from the cabin and Chastiser. The rapids intensified as they drifted farther along the river, the churning water pulling him under as if he were a rag in a washing machine. *Don't fight it. Relax.* Soon, he broke through the surface and gulped air. Scanning the surface, he searched for Brooklyn. Where was she?

She bobbed to the surface ten feet ahead of him as she cleared the next rapid. Another wave sucked him under. His lungs burned. Just when he thought he couldn't hold his breath any longer, the water spat him out.

He opened his eyes and looked around. They'd reached calmer water. It was a minor victory, since the current was still strong, and he was sure there would be more rapids around the bend. Brooklyn swam parallel to the current toward the opposite bank. Smart thinking, since they couldn't be sure if Chastiser had trailed them downstream.

Landon flipped onto his stomach and followed her. After what felt like an eternity, he neared the shoreline where Brooklyn lay on top of a boulder—one arm holding her in place and the other stretched toward him. Landon was sure if he grasped her helping hand he'd pull her into the water. He waved her away. She yelled at him, but the rumbling water in his ears prevented him from understanding her.

"Waterfall!" she yelled. "There's a waterfall. Give me your hand."

Her words penetrated his brain, and he reached toward her with his right arm, stretching as far as he could. She wrapped her hand around his wrist. He kicked and swam the remaining distance, one-armed. Reaching the bank, he pulled his upper body onto it and collapsed in the mud.

Brooklyn slid off the boulder and lay down beside him. "I've had enough exercise to last me for years."

He wheezed. "We…can't…stay here. Don't know… where shooter is." Using all the energy he could muster, he pushed to a seated position and reached for his gun. His holster was empty! When he'd placed his gun in its holster, he'd left the strap unfastened for easy access. The weapon must have floated away when they'd been dumped into the river. Sighing heavily, he stood and held out his hand to help Brooklyn to her feet.

In one fluid move, he pulled her upward until they stood face-to-face, inches apart. "Thank you for saving my life."

She threw her arms around his neck. "I thought…we were going to die."

I did, too. He returned her embrace, her hug recharging him. *Thank You, Lord, for protecting us.* "But we didn't. Now we need to figure out how to make our way back to the cabin so we can get my vehicle and get out of here."

"How did he find us? Where will we go?"

"I don't know. But I'll find a place he can't locate us." Reluctantly, he stepped out of her arms and looked around.

There would be no point trying to make their way back upstream. He had seen no way to cross the river on the portion they had traveled today. "We'll have to go downstream. Maybe we can find a way to cross to the other side."

"Will we have to hitchhike back?" Brooklyn's eyes widen. "We don't know what Chastiser looks like. What if *he* picks us up?"

"We'll be careful. But right now, our primary goal is to get out of these woods before dark." Landon laced his fingers with hers, caressing the back of her hand with his thumb. "Let's go."

He led her into the woods, staying close enough to see the riverbed but far enough that the shadows of the trees would hide their movements. A clap of thunder sounded overhead, and Brooklyn jumped ever so slightly. Landon tightened his grip on her hand, and she gave a slight squeeze. He prayed her trust in him wasn't misplaced. So far, he hadn't done a good job of keeping his promises to her. He'd allowed Chastiser to get too close, again.

EIGHT

Fifteen minutes later, a second round of storms moved into the area. Strong wind bent the trees sideways and rain pelted Brooklyn. "The storm is getting worse!"

"We need to find a place to wait it out." Landon looked around. "Unfortunately, I'm not familiar with the area."

"I remember my history teacher talking about caves in this area when I lived in Knotty Pines. Too bad I didn't ask him more questions about them. If I had, maybe I'd be able to find one now."

"You mentioned you lived in a foster home in the area. How old were you?"

"Ten when I moved here. Eleven when I left." Brooklyn searched their surroundings. Water to the left and trees to the right. Both dangerous to be around in lightning.

"We need to go deeper into the woods," Landon declared.

"Is that wise? Don't tall trees attract lightning?"

"They can, but we're not any safer standing here. Maybe we'll find one of those caves your teacher told you about. Or at least a dry place to wait out the storm." He grasped her hand. "The longer we stand around debating what to do, the stronger the storm is getting."

He pulled her into the woods, running. She matched his

pace, step for step. For once, she was thankful for her long legs. As a teen, she had despised being taller than all the boys and girls in her class. The teasing had been relentless. But what she had once seen as a flaw was a blessing today. As they plowed deeper into the woods, the trees provided some shelter from the blowing rain. After traveling about two hundred yards, she noticed a rock overhang protruding out of the side of the mountain.

She pointed. "Is that a cave, or just a large rock?"

"I'm not sure, but it looks like our best option for shelter."

As they drew near, it became obvious it was not a cave. Her first thought had been correct—it was a boulder that stuck out from the side of the mountain. At its highest, the space under the boulder was about seven feet high, narrowing as it went farther back to about three feet high.

Ducking, Landon led her as far under the rock as possible while standing. "It may not be much, but at least it's dry."

They both settled onto the ground, and then scooted backward as far as they could without hitting their heads on the rock.

"Do you think the storm has chased Chastiser away?"

"I sure hope so, but—" He shook his head.

"But…?"

A worried expression crossed his face. "He's getting desperate. When he shot at us as we left my house, he was targeting me. Today…"

"He didn't seem to care if he hit me," she finished for him.

Brooklyn watched as the trees swayed in the wind. One would bend to the right and the one beside it would bend to the left. She had never seen anything like that before. "Do you see what the wind is doing? I've—"

"Shh… Listen."

A roaring rumble sounded, growing louder and louder.

"Tornado! Lay flat!" Landon motioned for her to get down on the ground and scoot to the back of the crevice. "Wedge yourself against the rock and pray the wind doesn't suck us outside."

Jammed against the rock, she covered her ears with her palms, desperate to block out the sound. Landon scooted against her, blocking her from the outside, and wrapped his arms tightly around her.

Lord, cover us with Your protection. Don't let us be sucked into the tornado. A horrific thought hit. *And, please, don't let the rock we're hiding under break loose and crush us.*

The roaring sound intensified. Dirt and debris blew into Brooklyn's eyes. She squeezed her eyes closed and hid her face in the crook of Landon's neck, desperate to block the dust from her eyes and nose. He buried his face in her hair, and his arms tightened around her waist.

"Dear Heavenly Father, protect us—Your children. Please, keep us safe in the midst of this storm," he prayed aloud.

A sense of calm settled over her. She couldn't remember the last time someone had prayed for her, out loud, in her presence. The knowledge that no matter the outcome, she was covered in God's loving embrace and He was in control wrapped around her like a cocoon, silencing the chatter of the outside world.

Finally, the sound of the tornado quieted as the storm blew past them. Cautiously, she lifted her head and met Landon's gaze, their faces inches from one another. After several long seconds of staring at each other in silence, he lowered his head. His lips lightly touched hers, then all too soon, he pulled back.

Brooklyn's heart thudded in her ears. The last time

someone had kissed her, she'd been seventeen years old, and it had not been a pleasant experience at all. A month after she'd run away with Larry at sixteen, they'd met Nikki— a nineteen-year-old, more sophisticated girl—and she invited them to sleep on the couch in the apartment she shared with her boyfriend. It had been nice in the beginning, but then Nikki and her boyfriend, Phil, had started giving her drinks. The alcohol made Brooklyn feel grown-up and sophisticated. She was no longer being treated like a child. But then she started losing blocks of time and waking up in rooms with strange men. The third time it happened, Brooklyn realized she was being drugged.

She had begged Larry to run away with her again. This time to escape their new *friends*. He laughed at her and told her to stop being a baby. No one got a free ride in life and everything cost something. She was paying their rent for sleeping on the couch.

It had lasted for almost a year, because Brooklyn didn't think anyone cared about her or her circumstances. Then one night she'd had enough and refused to drink the drug-laced alcohol offered to her. Larry had beaten up Brooklyn and helped Phil lock her in a room with a man. That's the night she started plotting her escape.

Her body trembled. Whether from the kiss, her memories of her time as a runaway or what she and Landon had been through, she didn't know. Landon searched her face. She pushed against his chest. "I think it's safe for us to get out now. I'm feeling a little claustrophobic."

"Yeah, sure." He scrambled to the more open area under the rock.

She crawled out from the crevice where they had been wedged then stood and made her way to the opening and looked out. Tops of trees lay scattered about like the plastic logs in a child's building set. Thunder continued to rumble in the distance as the storm moved northeast of them, the sky clearing in the direction of the cabin.

Landon came to stand beside her. "That was the closest I've ever been to a tornado, and I will be happy if I never have to experience anything like that again."

"It was a bit too close for comfort." Her cheeks warmed. She wasn't talking only about the tornado. "I wonder if we have cell service yet."

"Doubtful." He removed his cell phone, glanced at it and slipped it back into his pocket. "No service."

She looked at her smart watch. "Yeah. Me either." Then, noting the time, she added, "It will be dark soon. We probably only have an hour to get out of these woods."

"Maybe we should climb to higher ground and try to get reception. Heath should be able to tell us how to find our way back to the cabin or at least send a search party."

They walked out from under the rock, turned and examined the face of the mountain. It wasn't more than thirty feet high and did not look like it would be an arduous climb.

"Stay here. I'll scale to the top." Landon reached for a handhold.

She reached for a handhold of her own. "You're not leaving me behind."

"It's too dangerous."

"Last time I checked, I'm a grown woman. I get to make my own decisions," she replied, pinning him with a glare that had always gotten her into trouble as a child for displaying too much attitude. Closing her eyes, she released a slow breath. Then she offered him a closed-lipped smile. "I appreciate all you're doing to keep me alive. And I'm thankful to have you here with me so I don't have to make all these decisions alone, but I don't take *orders* from you."

"Fair enough." He released his hold on the rock and dropped to the ground. "Do you have any climbing experience?"

She mimicked his move and landed, flat-footed, beside him. "I climbed my fair share of trees and rock piles as a child."

He raised an eyebrow. "This isn't a tree or a rock pile. It's the side of a mountain that goes straight up. Look…" Landon relaxed his stance, his posture softening. "If I have to worry about you as we climb, it's going to slow down the progress and take twice as long to reach the top."

Was he right? She'd always been staunchly independent. Even after Lillian had rescued her, Brooklyn hadn't wanted to be indebted to the older woman and had insisted Lillian allow her to contribute in some way so she felt like she was earning her keep. She had taken over the responsibilities of cooking and cleaning. It had bothered Lillian at first, since she was afraid it would appear that she was using Brooklyn for free child labor.

"What are you smiling about?"

She hadn't even realized she was doing so. Of course, she wasn't surprised. Thoughts of Lillian always lifted her spirits. "I'm thinking about all the times your aunt and I clashed over my desire to be independent and in control of my own choices."

"It wasn't my intention to take away your independence. If you feel that strongly about climbing to the top of this rock overhang with me, then I won't say another word." He reached out and placed a hand on her shoulder, and a jolt of electricity ran through her.

She bit her inner lip. What was wrong with her? She'd never had this kind of reaction to a man before. *When did I start thinking of Landon as a man?* Not that she hadn't always known he was a man, but she'd never thought of him in any context before. Until last year, he'd always just been Lillian's nephew who showed up at family events a few times a year.

Shaking her head, she pushed aside the thoughts as if she were sweeping away cobwebs. "No. That's okay. You made valid points. I'll wait here."

"If you're sure…"

"I am. I'll look around and see if I can tell how much damage the tornado caused." She sighed, wishing he'd go already and give her space to think without him being so close, touching her. "If there are a lot of trees down, it's likely to hinder our progress."

"Don't go too far, please." He dropped his hand from her shoulder and started his climb.

Brooklyn watched as he moved fluidly from one hand-hold and foothold to the next. He had been right. She would have slowed him down. And putting distance between them for even a few minutes was probably a good thing. Why had he kissed her? In all the years she'd known him, he'd never so much as given her a hug. At least, not until Lillian died and Brooklyn had been a crying mess. He'd held her tightly then and told her everything would be okay, that she had him to lean on. And she had done just that until the funeral was over. Then Lillian's lawyer had pulled them aside and informed them Lillian had left her agency to both of them. Sixty percent to Landon and forty to Brooklyn. It had been her desire that Landon have controlling interest, but that they make decisions together, continuing her work to save other young women who found themselves in the same situation Brooklyn had been in when she'd been younger.

She couldn't let Lillian down. So, she'd pulled herself together, resolved to be self-reliant. After that, she'd only cried in private, not willing to show any weakness. She and Landon had worked amicably ever since to build a business Lillian would be proud of.

Releasing a shaky breath, she turned away and surveyed her surroundings. The tornado had left a wide path of damage. Even if Landon could get a signal and contact Heath, she doubted they'd make it out of the woods tonight.

Almost there. He stretched as far as he could and felt for a handhold. Slipping his right hand into a small gap, he pulled with all his might and lifted the upper half of his body above the top of the boulder. Leaning across the giant rock, he flopped onto the surface, much like he'd seen seals at Sea World do when Aunt Lillian had taken him to Florida for his tenth birthday.

Rolling onto his back, he breathed deeply and forced air into his burning lungs. The climb had been much harder than he'd expected. Brooklyn should be glad she stayed on the ground. Pushing to his feet, he took in the tornado damage. It was hard to gauge how wide the path of destruction was, even from this height, but all the trees—as far as he could see—had had the tops ripped out of them. He leaned over and searched for Brooklyn. Where was she? "Brooklyn!"

There was a rustling of leaves in a pile of treetops to the right of him, and she stepped out into the open. Cupping her hands around her mouth, she yelled, "Do you have a signal?"

He pulled his phone out of his pocket. Two bars appeared. "Yes!"

Removing the phone from the protective plastic bag, he quickly punched in the number for the sheriff's office.

As soon as he gave his name, the receptionist patched him through to the sheriff.

"Landon, is everything all right?" Heath asked the second he answered the call.

"No. Chastiser found us. He set fire to the cabin—sorry. We escaped in the canoe. But he shot at us and hit the boat. It took on water and sank." Even in their dire situation, having to relay to Heath the damage that had occurred to the property he'd offered to them was excruciating. Landon would pay whatever was not covered by insurance. But for now, his concern had to be Brooklyn's safety. "We're in the woods downstream."

"Y'all need to find a place to take shelter. There are tornadoes near you."

"You're about ten minutes too late with that warning."

"What? Are either of you hurt?"

"No. We took shelter under a rock overhang. The tornado went right over us. It didn't touch down, but it took tops off the trees. There is a lot of debris."

He could hear Heath moving around on the other end of the line.

"You said a rock overhang? How far downstream are you?"

Landon buried his hand in his hair and scratched his head. "I'm not sure. We came ashore just before the waterfall. And we're maybe a mile and a half downstream from there now."

"Okay, give me a minute to look at the map. Hopefully, I can give you directions out of there."

"That would be great." Landon watched as Brooklyn climbed over a tree trunk and disappeared. He prayed she wouldn't wander too far. "Can you send someone to pick us up and take us back to the cabin? I want to get my tru—"

"That may not be possible. Three tornadoes have touched down this afternoon. My deputies are out searching for people who haven't been accounted for. I'll contact Jackson and see if he can pick you up, but he may not be able to reach you."

Dear Lord, forgive me for not thinking of others who have been impacted by the storm. "It's okay. We can hike back to the cabin if you can tell me how to cross this stream."

"Looks like you're about three miles from the bridge. Just keep going the way you have been. Call me when you get there. If I can send someone, I will." The sound of a chair moving came across the line. "If not, once you cross the bridge, you can follow the shoreline back upstream. But Landon—"

There was a beep, and the line went dead. He dialed Heath's number again, but the call would not go through. The cell strength bars had been replaced with the message SOS. The storm must have taken out the cell towers. At least, with the SOS feature, they should still be able to call 911 if they got into trouble. Since they weren't in immediate danger, and there was no way for anyone to reach them, there was no point in calling again.

He lay down on his stomach and looked over the side of the rocky ledge. "Brooklyn!"

"Yeah," she replied, crawling back over the log she'd disappeared behind a short while earlier.

"I need you to help guide me as I climb down, since I won't be able to see the footholds." He swung around so his legs dangled off the side, then he eased himself backward.

"There's a small rock a few inches to the right of your left foot."

Following her instructions, he settled his foot on the

rock. As he continued downward, following her verbal commands, it hit him that this was an exercise in trust. He could count on one hand how many people he'd trust with his life like this, but Brooklyn would be top of the list. *When did I come to rely on her so much, Lord? Does she trust me as much as I trust her?* Yesterday, he would have said she did. He'd thought they were growing closer, maybe even becoming true friends. After the events of the day, he wasn't so sure anymore. She'd seemed especially cool toward him after the tornado passed.

It's your own fault, dummy. You shouldn't have kissed her. It was a gut reaction after back-to-back near-death experiences. You can tell yourself that, but you know it's a lie. You almost kissed her back at the cabin. What was the excuse that time?

He shook his head to clear his mind. Would she think he was interested in dating her? No, she had to know that was the furthest thing from his mind.

Landon had made it perfectly clear over the past year that he was not interested in dating or settling down, rebuffing any flirtation from clients or other women. Besides, Brooklyn had admitted to knowing his childhood story. Surely, she understood there is no way he would dare to think he could be a husband or father…not after the example he'd had for a father.

He'd had friends—who he knew had good upbringings with loving parents who instilled in them a love of God and a firm foundation—share with him the challenges of being a good spouse and competent parent. For the first seven years of his life, no one had taken Landon to church. And he'd been raised by a man who preferred to spend his time drinking, gambling and watching sports to playing catch in the backyard with his only child. His mom had tried to make up for the way his dad ignored him. When his dad wasn't home, she would play games with Landon and let him help her cook. But the instant his dad walked through the door after work, she'd send Landon to play in his room to keep him from bothering his dad.

Landon hadn't had anyone show him how to be a husband or dad, but that was okay. He much preferred being a loner. He'd learned long ago the only person he could depend on was himself—and Aunt Lillian, but she was gone now.

Dropping the last couple of feet to the ground, he dusted off his hands and turned to Brooklyn. Time for what was likely the most strenuous hike of their lives. He just hoped the awkwardness between them would quickly dissipate and they could get back into the comradery they'd shared for the past few days.

NINE

"How bad is the damage? Were you able to make your way to the river?"

Brooklyn frowned. "There are trees and limbs scattered everywhere, so I didn't go all the way to the water. I wanted to stay close enough to hear you. In case you needed me."

She offered a closed-lip smile. Why did she feel like an awkward preteen trying to fit in at the lunch table? This was Landon. Her business partner. And friend—the closest thing she'd ever have to a brother.

Get it together. He didn't mean anything by the kiss. And could it even be classified as a kiss? It was barely a peck.

If she didn't snap out of the fog that had enveloped her, the hike out of here would be more emotionally torturous than the physical part of it. "Were you able to call Heath?"

"Yes." He nodded. "Unfortunately, we're on our own for a little longer."

"Why? Are we too far into the woods for someone to reach us?"

"I'll explain as we hike. It's going to get dark soon, so we need to get moving."

Landon placed a hand lightly on her back and guided her to the trail. Brooklyn swallowed the gasp that had wanted to escape when the familiar jolt of awareness raced through her body.

"Follow me." Moving ever so slightly away from his touch, she reached for a limb on the fallen tree in front of them and used it to pull herself over the trunk.

The trees that littered their path made it impossible for them to walk side by side, which was fine with her. Until she had time to examine the attraction she felt toward him, keeping space between them would be best. Once the authorities captured Chastiser, and Brooklyn and Landon returned to their ordinary lives, she was sure any attraction would dissipate.

Landon relayed his phone conversation with Heath as they slowly made their way back to the water in a game of follow-the-leader, with Brooklyn in the lead, which gave her a strange sense of satisfaction. Hopefully, Landon would see that she was still the strong, independent woman she'd always been. The fear she'd experienced during the tornado didn't define her. Heat warmed her cheeks as she recalled hugging him tightly—her face pressed into his neck and her ear listening to his heartbeat echoing hers. No wonder he'd kissed her.

Thinking about it now, the kiss had been more like a reassuring kiss a parent would give their frightened child. Well, she wasn't a child. And the sooner he realized it, the better. The small crack in her normal composure wouldn't have occurred if she hadn't already been running for her life. Puffing out a breath, she moved a low-hanging branch out of her path and stepped out of the woods and onto the riverbank.

The water level had risen. The rapids were angrier than they had been earlier. She turned to look downstream and gasped. The most amazing sunset she'd ever seen greeted her. The sun appeared to be sinking into the river. Streaks of orange, red, yellow, purple and blue stretched to the heavens, gray clouds in the distance behind them.

"God's artwork at its finest." Landon came to stand beside her, draping his arm across her shoulders.

This time, she did not step away from his touch. Instead, she accepted it as the friendly gesture she knew it was meant to be. *Thank You, Lord, for giving me someone to walk this path with me. Please, don't let anything happen to him because of his desire to protect me.*

"Making it back to the river took much longer than I thought it would," Landon said softly.

"It's going to be dark soon." She turned to see him scrub a hand over his face.

He met her gaze with weary eyes. "Yeah. I can't believe I didn't grab the backpack when we had to run. Of course, we probably would have lost it when we had to abandon ship. But those protein bars would have tasted—why are you smiling?" he demanded.

"You called a canoe a ship."

"That's just a figure of speech."

Her grin widened and she giggled.

"But you knew that." A smile split his face. "You're just trying to lighten the mood by making me laugh."

"It is the best medicine."

Landon's laughter mingled with her own. Soon, they were gasping for air as they struggled to control themselves. As much as she wished someone would rescue them, Brooklyn was thankful there wasn't anyone around to witness their outburst. Their laughter was more excessive than the comment had warranted, but stress, combined with mental and physical exhaustion, tended to cause exaggerated reactions.

"Okay…time to focus." She puffed out a slow breath, releasing the rest of her mirth with it. Then she turned to Landon. "Grabbing the backpack would have been nice, but we were slightly preoccupied trying to save ourselves."

"You're right. I can't go back and change things, so the best thing to do is focus on the situation we find ourselves in."

"You said we're three miles from the bridge?" For the first time since stepping out of the woods, she took in the storm damage along the riverbank. Just like it had been in the woods, a lot of trees and limbs were scattered in their path.

"It doesn't look like it's going to be an easy hike." He sighed. "I'm afraid we'll have to—"

"Spend the night in the woods," she finished the sentence for him. "Well, I'm sure things could always be worse. Why don't we see how far we can get before we look for a safe place to rest?"

Relief washed over his face. Had he been that worried that she would be upset over the situation they found themselves in? If anyone had a right to be angry, it was him, not Brooklyn. He wouldn't even be in this situation if it weren't for her.

"Do you want to lead the way?" he asked.

For some strange reason, she no longer felt a need to display her strength and independence. "No. You lead. I'll follow."

Where you lead, I will follow. Anywhere that you tell me… The lyrics to a television show's theme song popped into her head. Oh, great, an earworm. She vigorously shook her head.

"Are you okay?" Landon asked.

"Um… I'm fine." *Change the subject. Maybe it will help*

dislodge the earworm. "I just realized I don't know that much about your life outside of work and the few things Lillian shared about your time living with her."

"And what you read on the internet—" He pressed his lips together. "I'm sorry. I didn't mean that the way it sounded. And, to be perfectly honest, I tried to research your past, too, when I first heard about you. But I didn't find anything."

"I'm not surprised. After all, your aunt moved a stranger into her home. It's only natural that you'd want to know more about me."

She followed him around a log, her foot slipping into the cold water. He turned and caught her elbow before she could topple into the river.

"Thank you."

He offered a curt nod and turned back to the task at hand—fighting his way through the debris. "Of course, my search didn't reveal anything. Your foster care records would have been sealed. And when you ran away, I imagine you used a fake name so no one could find you."

Tears stung her eyes. She bowed her head, praying he didn't see them. Brooklyn would rather him believe the lies he'd told himself than the reality that had been her life. In fact, she had not used a fake name. She'd known there would be no need because no one cared what happened to her...not her foster parents or the caseworker. She was sure her exit from their lives had been a relief to them. Well, for all of them except her foster dad, who had enjoyed getting the check from the state each month.

They continued in silence until the shadows around them became so dark it would be reckless to continue. Landon pulled out his cell phone and clicked on the flashlight, scanning the area for a place they could rest comfortably. He should have stopped thirty minutes sooner before the light had completely faded. After his comment about not finding any trace of Brooklyn's history online, she'd clammed up. He'd felt like a heel for bringing up memories she obviously wanted to bury. It was bad enough his insistence that she gave the interview on the work Lillian's Legacy was doing had caused her to be targeted, once again, by Chastiser. She didn't need him reminding her of other dark memories. He understood the need to erase the past from your mind. When you had survived some horrific event, you could not allow yourself to wander into the dark recesses of your mind and relive it.

Brooklyn plowed into him. "Sorry."

He stumbled, took a step, regained his footing and turned to face her. "It's okay."

"I didn't realize you'd stopped. Guess I was focused on moving forward."

"No worries." He swung his light toward the woods. About thirty feet from where they stood, there was a flat, mossy area. Even though the rain had ended hours ago, it was sure to still be damp. Maybe he could take some of the fallen branches and make a mat of some sort to keep them off the ground. "It's too dark to continue. Let's see if we can make ourselves comfortable for the night."

Leading the way, Landon crossed to the area without rocks. He swept the beam of light in a wide arc. "This looks like our best option for a place to sleep." He propped his phone on a low-hanging tree limb. "Help me pull over some of these smaller branches covered with leaves. We can make a pallet out of them."

She scrunched her nose. "Won't that be lumpy?"

"Probably, but it will be drier than the mossy ground."

He grasped a small tree limb that lay nearby and dragged it to the flat area. "Hopefully, if we turn out the limbs—so only the leafy tips are over the area where we'll sleep—it won't be too bad."

Brooklyn nodded and started dragging limbs into a pile. After they had gathered twenty or so limbs, he arranged them over the mossy area while she stood out of the way.

"Okay, that should do it." He swept his hand, palm outward, toward the leaf pallet. "Would you like to test it?"

"Sure." She stepped cautiously onto the leafy carpet and settled onto the middle of it. "It's damp, but it's pretty comfortable. I've slept in worse places."

"Lik—" He swallowed the question he'd almost asked. This was the second time she'd said that. But it wasn't any of his business. If she wanted to share more details with him, she would. And if not, that was fine, too. His stomach growled, and he laughed. "Too bad finding food isn't as simple."

"Personally, I'd just be happy with something to drink." She turned toward the water. "I guess it wouldn't be wise to drink out of the river, huh?"

"I'm afraid not. But if we can't reach help by midday tomorrow, I'll probably take my chances and drink some of it."

Dear Lord, please, let us reach safety before we become too dehydrated. If we make it out of this alive, I will never venture anywhere in the woods without emergency supplies.

She frowned. "I'll let you test the water. If you drink some and don't suffer ill effects for a couple of hours, I'll know it's safe to drink."

"Sounds like a good plan to me." And it did, too. Landon would willingly sacrifice himself to save her, whether it meant taking a bullet or drinking tainted water. If it meant she'd be able to have the life she should have always had, the sacrifice would be worth it.

Brooklyn was the kindest, most giving person he'd ever met. She never complained about the hand she'd been dealt in life, and she always went above and beyond for the women who came to them for help. He would do whatever it took to keep her alive. He just prayed he didn't have to fend off a wild animal in the night, but even that would be preferable to facing Chastiser without a gun.

TEN

Snap! Crunch. Landon bolted upright and turned toward the sound that had awoken him, coming face-to-face with a startled doe and her fawn drinking from the river. The momma deer nudged her child. They leaped over a log and sprinted into the woods.

The early-morning sun was peeking above the mountains. Time to get moving. He stretched his arms over his head. *Ow, my poor aching back.* Rubbing his lower back, he looked around. Where was Brooklyn?

"Looking for me?" she asked from behind him.

He glanced over his shoulder and spotted her sitting on a boulder twenty feet away. "Good morning. Have you been awake long?"

"Not very long. I had just finished my morning prayer when the deer came along to drink from the river."

"That was a beautiful sight. I hate that I scared them away."

She giggled. "It looked like they scared you first."

"I've always been a light sleeper." Pushing to his feet, he made his way over to her. She scooted over, giving him room to sit down. "I'm surprised I didn't hear you get up."

Brooklyn searched his face. "I'm guessing experiences

in your early childhood are the reason you have always been a light sleeper."

He struggled not to squirm under her scrutiny. He'd never told anyone about the endless nights of fighting between his parents over his dad's drinking and gambling debts. His dad yelling and throwing things. Or the few times Landon had been brave enough to climb out of bed and run into his parents' room to throw his tiny frame between his dad's fist and his mom's body—desperate to stop the fight and his mom's silent sobs.

The last time Landon had intervened in the fight was the last night both of his parents had been alive. Landon's dad had been in such a rage, instead of pulling his punch as he always had and storming out of the house mumbling, he'd hit Landon square in the face, breaking his nose—blood spurting everywhere.

Landon's mom, who normally took whatever his dad dished out with minimal sound, had screamed. A neighbor—his dad's friend—had come over to intervene, taking Landon's dad back to his house to sleep it off while Landon's mom took him to the emergency room.

"Yeah, just as I figured." Having read his thoughts accurately, Brooklyn turned her gaze forward. "You didn't hear me get up because I'm talented at moving without making a sound. Comes from years of sneaking out of foster homes, trying to find my dad." She lifted one shoulder in a half shrug. "Which, when you think about it, is funny, since I never knew my dad. How can you find someone when you don't know their name or what they look like?"

There were no words he could offer. Even if he tried, he was sure she'd shrug off his sympathy. Because that's what he'd always done when anyone felt sorry for him. The silence stretched on until it felt deafening.

"I don't know about you, but I'm ready to get out of these woods. I'm sweaty and hungry." He stood and held out a hand to her. "What do you say? Are you ready for a long hike?"

Accepting his hand, she stood, a smile replacing the frown that had been on her face. "How far do you think it is to the bridge?"

"Heath said three miles from our starting point. Of course, that's an estimate. I figure we made it less than a mile last night, so maybe two, two and a half miles."

"Okay. Let's go." She turned downstream.

He put a hand on her arm and halted her. "We can't stay on the riverbank. We'll have to move into the woods."

"Won't that slow us down, with all the tree limbs down from the tornado?"

"Yes. But we're too exposed here. If Chastiser gets in a kayak and floats downstream, he'd be on us before we could hear him coming."

"I hadn't thought of that."

Placing a hand on her elbow, he helped guide her over and around the treetops and boulders scattered about the area.

"Are you sure we'll be hidden well enough? There are so many trees with the tops ripped out of them in the storm."

"I'm praying the wreckage will hide our movements. If he spots us, hopefully it won't be before we see him. And we'll have the trees and debris to hide behind if he shoots."

"Hopefully, you can shoot him before he can shoot one of us."

He hadn't wanted to worry her about their safety if the killer found them. But he had to be honest. "I can't use my weapon." Landon frowned.

"Why not?"

"I lost it in the river yesterday. I didn't properly secure it."

"Oh." She continued to pick her way through the downed trees, a solemn expression on her face.

The weight of disappointing her and causing her additional fear crushed him. His heart ached, just as it had when he'd been seven years old and his attempts to protect his mother had been like a pesky mosquito trying to sting a giant. *Lord, don't let me fail Brooklyn the same way I failed my mom.*

Two hours later, the sun beat down on them. Brooklyn wiped sweat off the back of her neck with her palm. She looked forward to a shower when they made it back to the cabin. Only, the cabin had likely burned to the ground. And even if it still stood, they wouldn't have time to shower and change into clean clothes. They had to get out of the area and find a new place to hide. But where? How far could they run to escape Chastiser?

"Do you need to stop and take a break?" Landon asked.

"No. Do you?" She glanced over her shoulder.

He frowned and shook his head. "I'm fine. But you suddenly slowed down. Any time you need to rest, just say so."

"I'm sorry. I guess I was deep in thought and not paying attention." She faced forward and picked up the pace.

"Want to talk about it?"

"Just wondering where we'll go once we get out of the woods."

"We'll call Heath. If he can't send someone to pick us up, we'll make our way back to the cabin. Hopefully, my vehicle is still drivable. If it is, we'll head back to Knoxville. Maybe Jackson has a safe house ready now."

"And if he doesn't?" Brooklyn hated to sound so pushy, but not knowing their next move was unnerving.

"I'll think of something. Don't—"

"Worry? Isn't that kind of easier said than done in a situation like this?"

"Yes. I'm sure it is. But trust me. I won't let you down again."

Again? When did he think he had let her down? When he took her in after her home was burned down? When he safely whisked her away from his home when the serial killer after her attacked them there? When he spent three days at a cabin in the middle of nowhere without cell service or internet, doing his best to keep her mind off the person who wanted her dead? When he taught her to canoe over rapids just in time for them to put it into action? When he had to float through the rapids to safety, losing his weapon in the process? When he covered her body with his as a tornado went overhead? When he slept on the hard ground, in the woods, instead of his warm bed in his home?

Lord, how do I let him know how thankful I am for him? That he's done more in six days to protect me than anyone in my past ever did, other than Lillian? If Chastiser succeeds in his mission and I don't make it out of this alive, Lord, I pray Landon doesn't blame himself.

She released a soft, quivering breath, praying the words she was about to say wouldn't sound like platitudes. "You *have not* let me down. Not once. I am thankful for you. And Lillian would be so proud of the actions…" Tears stung her eyes and her voice cracked. "You've taken to keep me safe. You didn't have to do any of it. After I left the hospital, you could have let me go to a hotel. None of this would have landed on your doorstep."

He placed a hand on her shoulder, halting her. "Let's sit for a minute."

Nodding, she sat on a large oak tree the storm had felled.

Landon settled beside her, his eyes scanning the river through the gaps in the trees. "I want you to know, if I didn't want to be here, right where I am, I wouldn't have volunteered to protect you."

"I know, but—"

His head jerked in her direction, the look in his eyes silencing her. "No buts. Hear my words. I…am…right… where… I…want…to…be. Not because I want to make Aunt Lillian proud—which is a given—but because I care about you and your safety. Like it or not, we are a family. You're stuck with me as an honorary—"

"Don't say *brother*." Her face warmed. Why did it matter if he saw her as a sister? Just yesterday, she'd thought of him as her honorary brother. What had changed? She was attracted to him. Brooklyn pushed her feelings aside. She'd have to examine them later.

He laughed. "Okay, I won't saddle you with the burden of being my honorary sister. How about cousins, twice removed?"

She smiled. "No matter what label we put on it, I'm glad we're friends."

"Yeah, me—" He put a finger to his lips, slipped off the log onto his knees and pulled her down alongside him.

Was that the sound of someone paddling? She peered through the leaves of the top half of a maple tree that had been ripped in half in the storm. Time inched by as they waited. Finally, a single kayak came into view. The paddler was dressed in full camouflage, including a face mask. It had to be Chastiser! Who else would need to disguise their identity while kayaking on a white-water river?

As the person drew closer, Landon put his hand on her head and pushed her to the ground. They lay quietly, listening to the sounds of the river and the paddle slicing the water.

"Kee-ah," a hawk squawked overhead.

The paddling sound halted. Landon raised up a few inches and peeked over the edge of the log. Brooklyn desperately wanted to ask him what he saw, but she was afraid to utter a single word. After several long minutes, Landon dropped beside her, lying on his back and looking toward the sky.

"He's gone," he whispered with a sigh.

She sat up and watched as the back of the kayak went around a bend in the river. "Do you think it was Chastiser?"

"Yes." Landon pulled himself up onto the log they'd sat on earlier. "What other reason would he have for going to so much trouble to hide his identity?"

"That was my thought, too." Wrapping her arms around her middle, she hugged herself tightly.

Landon slid onto his knees in front of her and pulled her into his arms. Unfolding her arms, she wiggled them out from between them and wrapped them around him, holding as tightly as she could. She'd never known a hug could absorb stress and fear the way his embrace did right then. Even though she knew they were crossing boundaries that, for the good of the agency and her heart, should not be crossed, she could not pull away. It was as if his hug was a battery, recharging her soul.

"Thank You, Lord."

"Amen," Landon whispered and pulled back.

She closed her eyes. She hadn't realized she'd spoken the words aloud. Not that she was ashamed of her faith, but her prayers—large or small—had always been something she'd preferred to keep between her and God.

"So." She opened her eyes and met his gaze. "Now what? Are you worried he'll be waiting for us downstream?"

He stood and, being ever the gentleman, helped her to her feet. "Worried? No. Concerned? Yes."

Brooklyn furrowed her brow. "What's the difference?"

"Aunt Lillian taught me that worry is an emotional reaction when we don't trust God's grace, power and love. On the other hand, concern is when we're not sure what the outcome may be and we proceed cautiously."

She'd never thought about it that way. "I like that philosophy. Thank you for sharing it with me."

"Come on, let's go." He took the lead and guided her through the maze of trees and limbs.

As they walked, she pondered over his words. Worrying was an area of her life that needed work. She'd always felt like she trusted God the way she should, but now she wondered if that were true. She watched as Landon moved a large limb out of their path.

Lord, I now realize worrying is what I do when I'm trying to control the narrative. I promise to always trust You and seek Your guidance. From the time You put Lillian in my life, until now, You've never let me down. From this point onward, when I catch myself worrying about something, I will redirect my thoughts and pray. And always seek Your will, not mine. Because no matter the outcome, I know You are, always have been and always will be, in control.

"Look! It's the bridge." Landon pointed at the wooden bridge that was about a hundred yards away. Heath hadn't told him it was a covered bridge.

Could Chastiser be hiding inside, waiting to ambush them? "Stay right behind me."

"Okay." She nodded.

They made their way up the embankment, staying low so the underbrush would provide cover. Thank goodness, there was no sign of the kayak or the kayaker along the river. However, he wasn't willing to take a chance with Brooklyn's life. They reached a short rock wall separating the slope leading from the river to the road.

"I need you to stay behind the rock wall. Stay low and out of sight."

Brooklyn's eyes widened. "You're going alone?"

"I'll be back to get you once I know it's all clear. That is, unless I run into Chastiser. In which case, I'll do everything in my power to distract him while you run away." And he would, too, without hesitation, if it meant keeping her safe and buying her time to get away.

She grasped his arm, tears glistening in her eyes. "No. Don't. You could get hurt."

"I'll be fine. But if you hear anything—the slightest indication something is wrong—get out of here as quickly as you can. Don't stop until you reach help. Do you understand?"

She threw her arms around his waist, laid her head against his chest and nodded. "Please be careful," she whispered.

Landon put a finger under her chin and tilted her face upward. No longer able to resist the pull he'd been feeling the last few days, he lowered his head and claimed her lips.

She returned his kiss with the same urgency. Several seconds later, he pulled back, grasped her wrists and removed her arms from his waist. Then he locked gazes with her.

"I mean it. Run and get help."

She nodded. A tear slid down her cheek. He brushed it away with his thumb, kissed the top of her head and climbed over the rock wall. The bridge was empty. An eerie feeling washed over him. The hairs on the back of his neck stood on end.

Shaking off the feeling of uneasiness, he walked the length of the wooden bridge deck. As he stepped out on the other side, he caught a glimpse of the kayak that had passed their hiding place earlier. It was two hundred yards away, and the man dressed in camouflage was struggling against the current, trying to turn it around. He had heard them!

Landon raced back across the bridge. He had to get to Brooklyn. The instant he stepped out of the opening, her head popped up, looking above the rock wall.

"What is it? Did you see him?"

"He's upstream. But he heard me on the bridge and is turning around. Come on. We have to hurry!" He grasped her hand and helped her across the low wall.

They raced across the bridge. As they came out on the other side, Landon caught sight of the camouflaged man lifting his gun and aiming at them.

"Go right, so the trees will provide cover." He charged into the ditch just as a gunshot sounded. A second and third shot came close behind.

They ran without stopping. Once they were out of clear sight of the river, he guided her back onto the edge of the road, where the surface was smoother and they could go faster.

Ten minutes later, gasping for breath, Brooklyn stopped short, bent at the waist and put her hands on her knees. "I need…air…"

As much as Landon wanted more distance between Brooklyn and Chastiser, they could not keep up the pace Landon had set. He looked down the road they had traveled. "I don't see him. Take a moment. It's unlikely he had a vehicle nearby. We would have seen it if he had. We can walk until we catch our breath."

"Thank you."

His lungs burned, and while he'd never admit it, he needed the break as much as she did. "Just be ready to dash into the trees if we need to hide."

Brooklyn fell into step beside him. He pulled out his phone and powered it on. Three bars. *Thank You, Lord.* He dialed the sheriff's number, then placed the phone on speaker.

"Landon," Heath said as soon as he answered. "Where are y'all?"

"About a mile and a half east of the covered bridge. Chastiser was in a kayak on the water. He saw us."

"How do you know it was Chastiser?"

"The bullets he fired at us were a giveaway."

There were muffled voices in the background. Heath was talking to someone. "Landon, if you follow the road you're on for another mile, you'll come to Smoky Hollow Road."

"The road your cabin is on?"

"Yes. Three miles down Smoky Hollow Road, you'll reach the dirt road that leads into the woods to the cabin. I know y'all are exhausted, but you need to keep moving. If you stop, you risk Chastiser reaching you before you can reach safety."

Irritation boiled inside him. He didn't need to be told to keep moving. What he needed was reinforcements—and someone to capture the killer. "What about an officer? Are you sending anyone to help us?"

"I have Deputy Moore en route to you. He just completed a prisoner transfer to Robbinsville. He's about an hour from you."

"Wouldn't it be faster to have the local police send someone?"

"Unfortunately, Sheriff Milton and his deputies are busy at the moment. The tornado that went over y'all touched down in Englewood before it reached you. Current reports say three dead and twelve injured, and there are still buildings and homes that need to be searched."

Brooklyn gasped. Landon clasped her hand in his free one.

"I understand. We'll stay off the road and make our way back to the cabin. Hopefully, Chastiser didn't mess with my Jeep. If it's drivable, we'll head to Barton Creek. We can come up with a plan and regroup after we get there."

Brooklyn elbowed him and mouthed, *May I say something?*

He nodded and handed her the phone.

"Heath?"

"Yes, Brooklyn?"

"I'm so sorry about the fire. Your cabin may be gone completely," Brooklyn said. "It seems like I'm bringing misfortune to all my friends."

Landon squeezed her hand.

"Brooklyn, this isn't your fault," Heath said. "We have insurance. The cabin can be replaced. I'm thankful you and Landon weren't harmed. Now, let's do what we can to keep y'all alive."

"On that note," Landon said, "we need to get moving. I'll call you once we're headed your way."

He disconnected the phone and slid it back into his pocket.

"We're going to run again, aren't we?" Brooklyn asked.

"If you think you can. It would help us get to the cabin faster."

"You run five miles every morning and have competed in several marathons. I don't—and have no plans to complete a marathon *ever*—but I'll do my best. It may be more of a jog than a run, but it still will be faster than walking."

"I promise not to complain." He smiled. "But we need to move off the road."

He guided her into the woods. Looking around, he assessed how difficult it would be to jog over the terrain. Thank goodness, it appeared the tornadoes had spared this area.

"Ready?"

"As I'll ever be." She took off at a steady jog. He was impressed.

Landon thought back to his last five-mile run six days ago, at the high school where he'd graduated eighteen years ago. When he'd finished, he'd walked one last lap as a cooldown while enjoying the beautiful sunrise—orange, red and gold streaks had painted the sky. One of the most breathtaking sunrises he'd ever witnessed. His phone had rung as he rounded the last curve. It had been the nurse notifying him Brooklyn was in the emergency room and he was in their files as her emergency contact. He had bolted for his car and raced to the hospital, never realizing how much that one phone call would turn his life upside down.

And as strange as it seemed, he was thankful for the turn his life had taken. Not the fact that Brooklyn was in danger and running for her life, but that he and she had grown closer, strengthening their ability to work as a team. Hopefully, the changes in their relationship would help them be better leaders for the foundation.

There was one issue he would need to address with her, though. The kiss. She had to know that it had been driven by the dangerous situation they found themselves in. It had not been something romantic but rather a need to feel human touch. Or at least that was what he had been told as a rookie by seasoned FBI agents who had experienced similar things when their protectees would romanticize their situation and convince themselves they'd fallen for the agent assigned to them. The only difference this time was that his protectee hadn't been the one to initiate the kiss. He had. Not once, but twice.

He needed to capture Chastiser before any more boundaries between them became blurred.

ELEVEN

Brooklyn's lungs burned and her legs ached. She didn't know how much longer she could keep up the pace, which was much slower than Landon was capable of on his own.

If they got out of this alive, she might ask to join him on his morning runs. It wouldn't hurt her to get into better shape. She cast a sideways glance in his direction. Sweat glistened on his skin and his muscles bulged as he pumped his arms. Her heart flip-flopped. Maybe working out with him wouldn't be a good idea. Much to her chagrin, she'd willingly accepted his kiss earlier—a kiss that had literally curled her toes, no less. Her only excuse was that she'd feared being separated from him, even for a short amount of time, afraid something might happen and she'd never see him again.

"Look—" Landon nodded to their left. "A cornfield. Let's go in. The tall stalks will hide our movements."

Apprehension snaked up her spine as she remembered the movie her mom had insisted they watch together when Brooklyn was eight. "Haven't you ever seen a scary movie? There are always monsters in a cornfield."

He smiled and slowed to a walk. "Hollywood monsters and real-life ones are different. Right now, I'm more concerned about monsters that could drive by and shoot us."

"You're right." Regret that she'd said anything washed

over her. She felt silly. Would she ever be able to forget—
and forgive—the things in her childhood that she'd allowed
to take up a bigger space in her brain than they deserved?

Landon slipped between two stalks of corn. And she followed, surprised to find the rows weren't well defined like
the ones she'd seen in the movie. Instead, the two of them
fought their way through dense cornstalks. Once they'd
gone only ten feet into the field, they could no longer see
the road, which meant no one could see them, either.

She released a breath, forcing her anxiety out with it. "This
was a good idea. But what kind of corn is this? The stalks
are brown. And why aren't there rows to walk between?"

"This is field corn. It's left in the field until it's hard
and dry, like this." He moved a cornstalk out of the way.
"Then it's harvested for animal feed, or renewable fuels
and things. So, it doesn't require as much tending as corn
that's grown for food. Hence, no obvious rows."

"Makes it harder to walk through."

"Also makes it easier to hide."

"True." A thought struck. "Heath said once we turned on
this road, we'd be about three miles from the cabin. If there
are cornfields here, do you think there's a house nearby?"

"I don't know. Maybe. When we drove to the cabin,
we came in on the other end of this road. There were a
few houses there, but they looked deserted, so they were
probably vacation rentals. And, as you know, we didn't
find any houses within a mile on either side of the cabin.
Could be the farmer lives miles away and this is just one
of his fields."

"Well, I'm thankful he put a field here. I hope it goes on
for a while, especially since it's giving us a chance to slow
our pace, and catch our breath."

He smiled back at her but didn't comment. They continued walking in the direction of the cabin, staying out of view of the road.

The sound of an approaching vehicle broke the silence. Landon touched her arm and motioned for her to squat. The vehicle stopped and her heart leaped. Brooklyn put a hand over her mouth, squelching the scream that wanted to be released. She locked eyes with Landon. After an excruciating amount of time, the vehicle continued on its way, driving in the opposite direction. They remained squatted until the sound of the vehicle's engine had grown faint.

"Do you think that was Chastiser?" she whispered.

"I don't know, but whoever it was seemed to be searching for something—or someone." He helped her stand.

Her feet and legs tingled as the circulation returned to them, but she bit her lip and refused to admit she was in pain. She would not prevent them from quickly putting more space between them and a vehicle that might belong to the killer.

They continued on their path without a word. She was sure Landon was as focused on listening for the vehicle to return as she was. Finally, they came to the edge of the field.

"Wait here," he instructed before stepping through the last row of corn and disappearing.

After several long minutes, she wondered if he was ever going to return. What was taking him so long?

He popped his head through two cornstalks to her right. "All clear."

She stepped out into the open and followed him as they raced across a span of about fifty feet between the corn and the woods. A gravel road ran the length of the cornfield, but she didn't see a house. It either sat far off the road, or Landon had been correct. This field was located away from the farmer's house and this was the access road he used to get his farming equipment in and out of the field.

The sound of a vehicle approaching spurred her forward, and she burst into the woods. Landon pulled her behind a large pine tree. They watched the road and listened. The sound grew until it was a thunderous rumble. A large combine harvester came into view, turned onto the gravel road they'd just crossed and immediately did a U-turn into the field, mowing down the stalks that had sheltered them.

The sound of the farming equipment muffled Brooklyn's gasp. If they hadn't cleared the field when they had, the machinery would have run them over—their bodies mangled. Landon pulled her deeper into the woods, forcing her to take her eyes off the sight and the *what-if* images flashing through her mind.

"That…we could have…"

"But we weren't," he said forcefully. "Be thankful. Don't think about all the ways the scenario could have turned out differently."

One thing she'd always admired about Landon was his ability to stay positive no matter the situation. If it weren't for him, she'd most likely have fallen into despair days ago and perished at the hands of Chastiser.

Be thankful. Don't think about all the ways the scenario could have turned out differently. It would benefit her to remember his words in the future when she had difficulty turning off her mind.

Lord, I'm a work in progress. I pray I can learn to be more positive like Landon. I'm sure his positive, never-give-up attitude and Your grace are the only reasons I'm still alive. Please, continue to protect us. Amen.

They reached the dirt drive that led to the cabin. There had been no signs of any vehicles on the road, but Landon couldn't be sure Chastiser hadn't circled around and wasn't waiting on them at the cabin. Even though it would slow their progress, it would be best if they remained in the shadows of the trees.

He knew Brooklyn was tired, hungry and most likely dehydrated. The last time either of them had had anything to eat or drink had been lunchtime yesterday. He'd done longer fasts than twenty-eight hours before, but he had planned them. And he'd drunk enough electrolytes to stay hydrated.

The way Brooklyn had handled everything that had transpired since Chastiser showed up at the cabin impressed Landon. How had the killer found them at the cabin, anyway? They'd had three days with no attempts on their lives. Even though he'd been trying to prepare Brooklyn for an eventual escape via the water, he'd truly thought they were safe at the cabin. As if the cabin was some sort of cocoon of protection. He should have known better. One of the first things his instructors had taught him at Quantico had been to expect the unexpected.

"How do you think he found us?" Brooklyn said, breaking into his thoughts with the exact question he'd been pondering.

"I'm not sure. As far as I know, the only people who knew we were here are Heath and Jackson Knight. I don't believe either of them is Chastiser."

"I don't, either."

"It doesn't mean one of them didn't let our location slip to someone they trusted."

"Do you think Chastiser is in law enforcement? Could he be one of Heath's deputies? Someone I've crossed paths with in Barton Creek since I moved there?"

"I guess it's possible. No one, other than me and Aunt Lillian, knew about your past run-in with Chastiser." He glanced at her. How did he say what he was thinking without it sounding like an insult?

"You look vastly different than you did when you were seventeen. As we all do," he rushed on before his words offended her. "You've grown into a beautiful, sophisticated woman who exudes confidence."

"Nice save." A smile quickly replaced her frown. "The thought that I might actually know—and possibly like—the person doing this is nauseating."

They reached the edge of the woods. He put out a hand, halting her from stepping out into the clearing, then scanned the area. His Jeep sat exactly where he'd parked it four days ago. On the front left side of the cabin, a window had been shattered and there were black soot marks. Thankfully, it looked like the two rounds of rain—one before the attack and one after—had prevented the entire cabin from burning down.

"I have to go inside to get my keys. Stay hidden until I get back."

She nodded, her eyes rounding. He hated to leave her side, even for a second, but he didn't want her out in the open any more than necessary. Darting out of the woods, he ran to the back steps, raced up them and barged into the cabin—the door still unlocked. The inside of the cabin appeared to be untouched by the fire. He charged down the hall to the bedroom where he'd slept. Nothing seemed out of place. It seemed, once Chastiser realized they'd escaped, he'd left without messing with anything else.

Snatching his keys off the bedside table, he quickly ran back to the kitchen and grabbed a banana and two bottles of water. Then he stepped outside and crossed to his vehicle. Hitting the unlock button on his fob, he hopped in, placing the water bottles into the cup holders and dumping the fruit onto the center console. Then he pressed on the brake and started the engine. It sounded fine, and everything seemed to be in working order. Rolling down the driver's side window, he waved for Brooklyn to come out of hiding.

She raced across the small stretch of lawn, climbed inside the Jeep and clicked her seat belt in place. "I guess you didn't want to waste time gathering our things, huh?"

"It didn't seem important." Putting the vehicle into Drive, he made a big circle and headed up the long dirt drive. "I did grab water and a banana."

She picked up the banana, peeled the skin, pinched off half the fruit and held it out to him.

"You eat it. I'm fine."

"Nothing doing. We split it. Besides, if I eat too much too quickly, it will make me sick. I'm not used to fasting."

He accepted the offering. "I'm sorry I didn't grab any of your things."

"It can all be replaced. But I would have liked my cell phone. That's the second one I've lost this week."

"Do you want me to turn around?" They were nearing the end of the long driveway.

"No! We managed to get away. We're not going back. Maybe Heath can have someone pick it up for me. It won't hurt me to disconnect for a few days."

"I really am sorry. If we can't get it returned to you soon, I'll buy you a replacement. Everything else, we'll pick up on our way to our next location."

"Any ideas where we can go that will be safe?"

He desperately wanted to tell her he had a dozen ideas of safe locations and a rock-solid plan for keeping her alive. But he wouldn't be able to convince himself of such a lie, so why would he believe he could convince her? "I'm sure Jackson and Heath can come up with a safe place. Let's focus on getting to Barton Creek first. Then we can worry about where to go from there."

She gasped. "We forgot about the deputy that Heath sent to assist us. Should we be leaving on our own?"

"Heath had said the deputy was only an hour away. That was almost ninety minutes ago." Landon stopped at the end of the drive and turned left onto Smoky Hollow Road, heading toward Barton Creek. "He could have run into some trouble along the way—or there could be storm damage blocking his path. Either way, the more distance we can put between us and the cabin, the better I'll feel."

"I guess you're right. Besides, once we make it to the Knotty Pines city limits, we should have cell service. Then I can call Heath to let him know what's happened." She turned and looked out the passenger side window. "I wonder how much Knotty Pines has changed since I lived there twenty-two years ago? I didn't pay much attention when we drove to the cabin on Wednesday after the hotel fire."

He needed to get her mind off all the attacks she'd endured, even if only for a little while. "Tell me about your time in Knotty Pines. You sound almost wistful when you mention it. How old were you when you lived here? Have you visited the area since?"

"I was a terrified ten-year-old when I arrived. I'd just been taken from my mom. And I'd never spent a night away from her." Brooklyn sighed. "She may not have been perfect, but she was still my mom. And I loved her."

He reached across and squeezed her hand. One day, he'd tell her about his imperfect parents and how he'd cried himself to sleep for six months, still missing them—both.

"I wasn't sure what to expect at a foster home, but Mrs. Jane took me in just like I was one of her own. She was the grandmother I'd never had. Sixty-five years old and as spry as a thirty-year-old. She took good care of me and made sure I knew I was loved. For the first time in my life, I had someone who took me to church, encouraged me to do right and to study hard, who told me I could be anything I wanted to be when I grew up."

"She sounds like a nice person. When was the last time you saw her?"

"Eight months after I moved in…she had a heart attack and died." Her voice cracked. "And I left here, a jaded eleven-year-old."

His heart broke for her. He never should have asked her to tell him about that time in her life. Why had he pried? If she'd wanted him to know, she would have volunteered the information.

She turned toward him and smiled. "Mrs. Jane set the bar high for how a foster parent should treat a child in their care. Maybe that's why, when my next foster parents didn't seem as loving, I started acting out. Turned into a real difficult child."

"I can't imagine that."

"It's true. The sad thing is my second set of foster parents weren't bad people. They just weren't Mrs. Jane. And, after two months of my horrible behavior, they told my caseworker I needed to be moved. They didn't want the other two foster children in their care to be influenced by my attitude." She pursed her lips. "If I had realized, with every move, my situation would get worse and worse, I would have behaved better and stayed with the Vance family. I think they would have warmed to me, eventually."

The slope of the mountain steepened, causing the Jeep to gain speed. Landon pressed on the brake. Nothing happened. He tightened his grip on the steering wheel and pumped the brakes again, glancing at the speedometer.

Sixty-one miles per hour felt more like ninety on the curvy mountain road.

"Why aren't we slowing down?" Brooklyn grasped the grab bar above the door with her right hand and clutched the center console with her left.

"The brakes aren't working." He pumped them again. Still nothing.

A diamond-shaped yellow warning sign with a squiggly arrow pointing upward came into view, showing they were fast approaching the section of road with back-to-back curves. He had to slow the vehicle. "Hang on!"

White knuckling the steering wheel, he pressed on the clutch and shifted from sixth gear to fifth. The engine revved, but the vehicle slowed. Sixty… Fifty-nine… Fifty-eight… Fifty-seven.

Midway through the first curve, he shifted into fourth gear. The vehicle continued to slow… Fifty… Forty-nine… Forty-eight…

"It's working," Brooklyn said, barely above a whisper.

"For now. But the last curve is a lot sharper." He blew out a breath. "Pray this works."

"Believe me, I've been praying this entire time. I won't stop. Until this vehicle is parked."

He shifted into third, gripped the wheel tightly and flew around the curve twenty miles per hour faster than the recommended posted speed limit of fifteen miles per hour. The vehicle tilted—the driver's side tires coming off the pavement several inches. The curve straightened, and the Jeep righted itself—the tires dropping back onto the asphalt with a jolt.

Brooklyn breathed an audible sigh of relief. His heart beat gradually returned to a normal rhythm.

They made it to the bottom of the mountain. He drifted

onto the shoulder of the road. Grasping the emergency hand brake, he pressed in the release button on the end and slowly pulled upward. The Jeep came to a stop. He crossed his arms over the top of the steering wheel and rested his forehead on them, taking several steadying breaths.

Sitting upright, he turned toward Brooklyn and she threw her arms around him.

"You did it! You saved us. I've never seen anything like that in my life." Her warm breath tickled his neck as the words came tumbling out. "You were so calm."

"I'm glad it looked that way on the outside, because I promise you, on the inside, I was quaking." Wrapping his arms tightly around her, he drew her even closer, ignoring the console between them that bit into his side, gave her one last quick squeeze then gently pushed her away. "I need to call Heath and see what happened to that deputy. And we'll need a tow truck. It's too dangerous to drive the vehicle now."

"What do you think caused the brakes to fail?"

"I imagine, once a mechanic looks it over, we'll discover that Chastiser tampered with them."

Landon should have looked the vehicle over before driving it. The urgency to get Brooklyn to safety and the relief he'd felt seeing the vehicle unharmed by the fire and the tornado had clouded his judgment. He could not allow that to happen again.

Taking his phone out, he pulled up his call history and tapped Heath's number. He prayed the sheriff had someone who could reach them before Chastiser found them stranded on the side of the road.

TWELVE

"Did the tow truck driver say how long it would take him to get here?" Brooklyn asked.

"He said he was ten minutes away." Landon glanced at his cell phone. "That was fifteen minutes ago. I imagine the storm damage cleanup is causing a lot of road issues."

"I guess that's to be expected. From what Heath said, it sounded like the tornado wiped out an entire neighborhood."

"Yes. And I was relieved to hear that his deputy didn't run into any roadblocks reaching us, but that he was delayed because a husband whose wife was in labor flagged him down. At least we know the roads should be clear from here to Barton Creek." He glanced up and down the road. "If only the tow truck would arrive. It makes me nervous sitting out in the open like this."

His admission was the first time she'd known he was feeling nervous or anxious while they had been on the run. She'd been so worried about her own emotions that she hadn't given any thought to his. If they avoided Chastiser until the FBI captured him, she would owe Landon her deepest gratitude. Maybe she could take on more responsibilities with the agency and the foundation. Help ease his load. The past year, she'd left all the decisions up to him, even when he asked for her input. It was time she stopped shirking her responsibilities to him and to Lillian's memory.

The sound of a vehicle approaching from the direction of the small town drew their attention.

"Get down until we know who it is," Landon slipped his hand inside his jacket and unsnapped his holster, momentarily forgetting his gun wasn't there. He balled his fist and placed it on the steering wheel.

Brooklyn slid down in the seat until she could barely see over the dashboard. A big, red truck with the words *Al's Garage & Wrecker Service* painted on the side pulled to a stop beside them.

The driver—a man in his late fifties with silver hair and a beard—rolled down his window. "You the one who called for a wrecker?"

"Yes, sir." Landon got out of the Jeep and stood on the edge of the road talking to the driver. "My name is Landon Wentworth. I live in Knoxville. Was vacationing in the area."

Brooklyn settled herself back onto her seat.

"Nice to meet ya. I'm Albert Lennon—Al to my friends. Owner of Al's Garage and Wrecker Service. What do you think is wrong with your vehicle?"

"The brakes went out on me. We barely made it off the mountain. Was touch and go there for a minute."

"All righty. Let me get 'er hooked up, and we'll tow 'er to the shop." Al drove past them and did a U-turn. Then he pulled in front of them and backed up until his bumper was only inches from the bumper of the Jeep.

Landon rounded the back of the vehicle and opened Brooklyn's door, holding his hand out to assist her on the uneven ground.

She gladly accepted. "Thank you."

"Why don't you sit on the bank while we wait for him to finish? But stay where the wrecker blocks you from any oncoming traffic, okay?"

"Okay." She went halfway up the embankment and sat on the ground. She was thankful it was dry despite all the rain from the day before.

Landon stood a few feet in front of her, his arms crossed, watching the tow truck driver as Al hooked a big chain on a pulley system onto the front of the Jeep.

"Beep! Beep!"

Brooklyn jumped at the sound of a car horn. She'd been so engrossed in the activity in front of her she'd missed seeing the older model, large blue sedan pull up beside the tow truck.

Al smiled and lifted a hand in greeting but didn't let it interrupt the job at hand.

The driver of the sedan rolled down the passenger side window and remained in the road, with the engine running. Once the Jeep was loaded and secured, Al walked over to talk to the man behind the wheel. Brooklyn couldn't make out what they were saying, but she caught glimpses of the man driving the sedan looking at her and Landon.

A few minutes later, Al walked over to them. "Okay, folks. I'm ready to roll. If y'all don't mind riding with Joseph, he said he'd be happy to give you a lift."

"Um… I appreciate his hospitality, but if it's all the same, we'll ride with you." Landon dropped his arms to his side.

Brooklyn agreed. The fewer people they interacted with, the better. Besides, the man in the car was a stranger. At least Al was at the scene because they'd called him, not because he'd happened by.

"Suit yourself. But you're gonna be mighty cramped in

the cab of my truck. You'll have to share the space with my coon dog, Boone."

"We'll be fine," Landon insisted.

"Okay, you can get on in the cab. I'll let Mr. Caldwell know you appreciate his offer but you're going to pass."

Brooklyn, who had stood to walk to the wrecker, paused midstride. "Did you say Caldwell? Mr. Joseph Caldwell?"

"Yes, ma'am." The tow truck driver pushed his baseball cap back and scratched the top of his head. "Do you know him?"

"Does he have a daughter named Peggy?"

"Yes, but—"

Joseph Caldwell laid on his horn, motioning for Al to come over to his vehicle, and the rest of the tow truck driver's sentence was lost.

"Do you know the man in the car?" Landon asked, a frown on his face.

"Yes. Or I did…a long time ago. The Caldwells were Mrs. Jane's closest neighbors. His daughter, Peggy, was sixteen months older and two grades ahead of me in school. But she was the first friend I made after moving here. Being a foster kid, I wasn't allowed to go to other people's homes for sleepovers but Mrs. Jane allowed Peggy to spend the night once in a while." She frowned. "It was the closest I ever came to feeling like I had a sister. I missed Peggy as much as Mrs. Jane when I had to be moved. Back then, I didn't have social media or a cell phone, so there was no way to stay in touch."

The blue sedan pulled off the road, and Mr. Caldwell exited the vehicle. He'd aged in the twenty-one years since she'd last seen him. His black hair had turned white, and he balanced himself with a cane—one with four small legs on the bottom for added stability. But, with his silvery blue eyes and the scar that ran down one side of his face, she would have recognized him anywhere. A former park ranger, he'd told her how early in his career, he'd saved a young mother and her child from a black bear after they'd gotten too close trying to take a picture. He'd put himself between the family and the bear, but before he could get his bear spray out of its holder, the animal had swiped at him.

The older man ambled his way over to them. "Al said you know me. Do I know you?"

"Yes, sir, Mr. Caldwell. But you may not remember me. It's been more than twenty years since we last saw each other. I lived with Mrs. Jane for a short while before she passed away."

"Hope?" He squinted at her. "No. You don't look like Hope. She had a gap in her teeth a—"

"Braces." She smiled, her heart about to burst with happiness. Someone from her childhood remembered her.

"Huh?"

"I wore braces for three years." Wearing braces on her teeth in her twenties hadn't been a pleasant experience, but she'd been determined to change her look as much as she could. So, once she'd graduated college and started earning her own money, she'd scheduled an appointment with an orthodontist. She still slept in a retainer at night. There was no way she was going to allow her teeth to shift and become crooked again after all the money she'd spent to straighten them.

"Hope's hair was lighter. More of a strawberry blond."

"It darkened to this auburn color as I got older. I guess I stopped spending as much time outside in the sun."

"I can't believe, after all these years, little Hope has come back to Knotty Pines." He turned to Landon, then back to Brooklyn. "Is this your husband?"

"No, sir. This is my…" What was Landon to her? A week ago, she would have introduced him as her boss because that was the way she'd thought of him for the past year. Even though Lillian had left Brooklyn shares in the business and Landon had continually insisted he wasn't her boss, he held majority ownership. Perhaps, the title had been her way of keeping a boundary between them. But that wasn't the way she felt now. They were business partners, coworkers, friends. And perhaps more?

"My name is Landon." He glanced at her with a raised eyebrow. Then held out his hand to Mr. Caldwell. "I'm *Hope's* friend. Nice to meet you."

She needed to get herself together. Stumbling and fumbling like this would draw more attention to them. They did not need anyone asking questions—not even a childhood friend's dad.

Standing to the side, Landon quietly listened to Brooklyn and Mr. Caldwell discussing old times. The tow truck driver came over to him. "Where do you want me to take your vehicle?"

Landon glanced at Al. "I just figured you'd take it to your shop."

The older man pushed his cap back and scratched his head as he had earlier. "Well, I can, but you see, with the tornado damage and cleanup underway, it will be several days before I can get to it."

"You don't even know what's wrong with it. It could just need brake fluid."

"Don't matter. My neighbors are in need. Assisting them will come before any mechanic jobs." The man assessed him with knowing eyes. "I was helping my brother clear debris off his roof when I got the call you needed to be towed. Wouldn't have taken the call, but don't want anyone stranded on the side of the road. Too many evil people in this world who would harm two nice folks like you. I see it on the news all the time. And I'm not naive enough to think it can't happen in my small town."

"Well, folks," Mr. Caldwell said. "Guess I'll get outta y'all's way. I'll send your love to Peggy. I'm sure she'll be jealous when I tell her I saw you." He pulled Brooklyn into an embrace and locked eyes with the tow truck driver. A look Landon couldn't decipher passed between them.

Mr. Caldwell stepped back. "Al, don't fill these folks' heads with gossip when you drive them to the shop. They don't want, nor need, to know all the secrets of our little town."

"Don't be spreading lies, Joseph. You know I ain't no gossip."

"Don't get offended. You know I think highly of you. You've always been a good friend. But even you have to admit, sometimes you overshare your neighbors' business when no one *asked*." Mr. Caldwell laughed, clapped Al on the back, then turned to Landon. "I'm sure we'll see each other again."

"It was nice to meet you, sir." Landon reached back and grasped Brooklyn's hand. A sudden need to feel a connection to her overwhelmed him. He'd never dreamed of meeting someone she'd known when she was a child. Someone who had been like family to her for a brief time in her life. A sudden jealousy came over him as he pictured Brooklyn in pigtails and overalls. These two shared memories he'd never experience with Brooklyn. He wished he'd known her when she was younger.

"Well, if you won't accept my ride, guess I'll get out of

your way." Mr. Caldwell glanced at their locked hands and shuffled toward his vehicle.

"Okay." Crossing his arms over his chest, Al turned to Landon. "Where do you want me to take it?"

"I guess the best thing to do is take it to the garage in Barton Creek."

"If you're going that far, you may as well ride with me." Mr. Caldwell had paused and leaned on the trunk of his vehicle. "Spending almost an hour crammed in the wrecker's cab with Al's hound will be horrible on your backs. That dog doesn't understand personal space."

Al chuckled. "That's true. He sure loves to lie on your lap and get his ears scratched."

Brooklyn looked at Landon, fear in her eyes. He knew she had a small scar on her finger from being bitten by a puppy at one of her foster homes, but he'd never known her to be afraid of dogs.

"Would it hurt to accept a lift?" she whispered. "It'd be nice to have more time to catch up."

"Okay." Landon released a soft breath. "Mr. Caldwell, if you're sure it's not too much trouble, we'd be happy to accept the ride."

A smile split the elderly man's face. "No trouble at all."

Landon gave Al his contact information to give to the garage in Barton Creek when he dropped off the Jeep. Then he sent a quick text to Heath.

Having the Jeep towed to the garage in Barton Creek. Brooklyn and I are being given a ride to your office by Joseph Caldwell. The father of a childhood friend. Should be there in forty-five minutes.

His phone dinged with a reply almost instantly.

Are you sure it's wise to ride with a stranger?

Landon's fingers flew over the phone screen.

I'm praying it is. Don't have much choice. He's in his early seventies and walks with a cane. No red flags. Will stay on guard.

Heath replied with a thumbs-up emoji, and Landon put his phone away. The battery was in the red. He hoped it would last until they made it to the sheriff's office and he could plug it in to recharge.

Al pulled his tow truck onto the road and waved as he drove away. Landon jogged over to the blue sedan, thankful Brooklyn still stood outside even though Mr. Caldwell had already settled himself behind the wheel.

She searched his face as he approached. "Everything okay?"

"Yeah. I was just texting Heath to let him know what was going on. Do you want to sit in the front?"

"I thought we'd both sit in back. If that's okay?"

Relief washed over him. Even though, with his clear physical restrictions, it was unlikely Mr. Caldwell was Chastiser, Landon wanted to keep Brooklyn close to his side. And sitting in the back seat would allow him a chance to study the man giving them a lift.

He held open the door and allowed Brooklyn to slip inside before him. Once they were settled, with their seat belts fastened, Mr. Caldwell started the vehicle, smiled at them in the rearview mirror and took off in the direction the tow truck—which was now out of sight—had gone.

"What are you kids doing out in this area? We don't see

many tourists out here. Most people want to stay in Pigeon Forge or Gatlinburg."

Brooklyn looked at Landon and gave a slight jerk of her head toward Mr. Caldwell, obviously wanting him to take the lead on any conversation. Was she afraid of saying the wrong thing and giving away too much information? He laced his fingers with hers, his heart warming at the gesture. She trusted him. And he trusted her. There was no one he'd rather have by his side, no matter the situation.

Lord, I'll have to examine my feelings and what they mean once we are no longer in danger, but for now, please help me stay focused on keeping her safe.

"We needed a break from the daily challenges life was throwing our way. Decided it would be good to spend time in nature."

"Yeah? What'd y'all do while you were here?"

"We spent time on the river and camped under the stars."

Brooklyn smiled—her lips pressed together.

"I used to enjoy things like that when I was young. Can't do much of that anymore. Not since my injury. Rockslide in the park, twelve years ago. Happened sudden. Boulder slammed into me. Broke my hip and leg." Mr. Caldwell pressed down on the gas pedal, and the vehicle sped up.

They passed a speed limit sign that read forty-five miles per hour. Landon leaned forward, catching sight of the speedometer. Fifty-two. He needed to change the subject. Maybe if they talked about something less distressing to the older man, he'd snap out of his semitrance and realize he was driving too fast.

"Thank you for offering to drive us to Barton Creek," Landon said. "I hope it isn't too far out of your way."

"It's not," Mr. Caldwell replied, his speed not slowing.

"Do you still live in the same place?" Brooklyn inquired.

"Yes. Just me and Peggy now. Lena left eighteen years ago."

His wife, Brooklyn mouthed.

Landon hated small talk, but a long, silent car ride seemed more awkward. "It's nice your daughter has stayed close by all these years."

"Peggy won't ever leave me." Mr. Caldwell looked in the rearview mirror and locked eyes with Landon before glancing at the dashboard. "Oh my. Didn't realize I was speeding." He slowed the vehicle.

"It's easy to get distracted while talking." Brooklyn squeezed Landon's hand. "We'll stop peppering you with questions."

They rode in silence for the next ten minutes. Suddenly, the speed of the vehicle dropped. Landon leaned forward. The speedometer registered twenty miles per hour. "What's wrong? Why are you slowing down?"

Mr. Caldwell looked at him—a blank stare on his face—and the vehicle swerved into the other lane.

Brooklyn gasped. "Truck!"

A delivery truck had topped the hill in front of them and was heading straight for them. Landon unfastened his seat belt, leaned across the seat, grasped the steering wheel and guided the vehicle back into the right lane.

Brooklyn leaned forward. "Mr. Caldwell, are you okay?"

"What? Yeah. No. I'm fine." He swatted Landon's arm. "What are you doing? Get your hands off the wheel."

Climbing into the front, Landon quickly settled onto the bench seat and fastened his seat. "I was saving our lives. What happened? You zoned out."

"I uh…just felt lightheaded…for a minute… I'm fine." Mr. Caldwell pressed on the gas and the vehicle climbed in speed until it reached the posted speed limit.

Was the elder man experiencing some type of medical

emergency? Landon had heard the expression *look right through you*, but he'd never experienced someone doing that until just now. Could Mr. Caldwell have had a seizure?

He watched as the older man drove, his hands shaking on the steering wheel.

"You're not fine," Landon insisted. "Pull over and let me drive."

Mr. Caldwell glanced at him, sighed and pulled the vehicle onto the shoulder of the road.

Landon wasn't sure what had just transpired, but he knew one thing for sure. Allowing this elderly gentleman to give them a ride had put him in a position where he'd have to protect two people if Chastiser showed up. And he didn't have a gun.

Shame washed over him. *Lord, forgive me. Instead of bemoaning the situation, I should be thankful Mr. Caldwell wasn't driving alone when he zoned out just now. If he had been, the results could have been the loss of his life and others on the road. But, please, let me get him to a medical care center and Brooklyn to a safe house without incident.*

THIRTEEN

As soon as the car stopped, Brooklyn scrambled out of the back seat and opened the driver's door. "Are you okay? What happened?"

Her friend's father swung his legs out of the vehicle and gave her a half smile. "I'm fine, dear. I'm sure it's just a mild drop in my blood sugar. I've had a few episodes lately, but I have an appointment with my doctor tomorrow. As soon as I drop you two off at the sheriff's office, I'll stop at a convenience store and get something to eat."

Had it been a hypoglycemic episode? She didn't know much about low blood sugar, but she knew it could be dangerous if it dropped too low. How much time did they have to get it up before it became critical? Brooklyn looked up at Landon, who'd rounded the front of the vehicle and stood on the other side of the door. He motioned her to move aside.

"Let me help Mr. Caldwell into the passenger seat. Then I'll drive us to the nearest gas station, where we can get him something to bring his sugar up." He leaned in and grasped the man by his upper arm, offering support so Mr. Caldwell could stand. "Pop the trunk and grab his cane."

"No. Don't. I'm fine. Stop fussing over me like I'm some helpless person." He shuffled around the open back door and dropped onto the seat, looking up at them determined look on his face. "I can sit in the back seat."

Once Mr. Caldwell's legs were inside the vehicle, Landon closed the door and pulled Brooklyn to the back of the vehicle. "Are you comfortable driving?"

"Yes. Why?" She furrowed her brows. Was he still concerned that Mr. Caldwell could be dangerous? Surely not.

"I thought I'd sit in the back seat with him in case he has another episode. I'm not sure what help I can be until we can get him something to eat, but I'm stronger than you. If he collapsed onto me, I could assist him."

Her heart swelled. Landon was a good guy, always thinking of others. "Okay."

He went right, and she went left. Once they had both slid into their respective seats and fastened their seat belts, she started the vehicle and pulled out onto the mostly deserted highway. They had only seen two vehicles in the past ten minutes. She hadn't traveled this road in years, but she remembered it always being a thoroughfare, connecting this section of the state to the Smoky Mountains tourist attractions. And while it would never compare to the congested traffic found on a busy city street, she couldn't remember ever seeing so few vehicles traveling on it. Was the storm damage blocking the flow or had the newer bypass highways made this a forgotten area?

She glanced in the rearview mirror.

Mr. Caldwell had a sullen look on his face while Landon sat, slightly turned, observing him. "Where's the nearest gas station or fast-food restaurant?"

"There ain't any. At least not until you get closer to Barton Creek. About twenty miles," Mr. Caldwell grumbled.

"What happened to the Corner Quick Stop? I remember Mrs. Jane stopping there to get gas and buy me snacks after school."

"Closed. Just like the only restaurant in town. Everything around here is slowly dying out. Just like the residents." The elderly man looked out his side window. "It's what happens when too many of the youth get wild ideas and abandon a town. Turning their backs on God and the solid foundation their parents tried to give them in life."

Brooklyn had never known Mr. Caldwell to talk so negatively. What had brought such bitterness into his life? Was it because his wife had left him? No, he'd only mentioned the youth in the town. Could Peggy have been one that turned her back on her upbringing? That didn't make sense. He'd said Peggy lived with him and would never leave. Did that mean some man had broken her heart, and she'd remained single like Brooklyn?

A smile pulled up the corners of her lips. A long time ago, they'd dreamed of growing up and living in a duplex, side by side. Brooklyn would have a dog and Peggy would have two cats. They'd all sit on the porch drinking fruit punch—might have to change that to coffee now that she was older—and people watch. Peggy had loved to watch people and make up stories about them. She was one of the most creative thinkers Brooklyn had ever known.

"Sometimes young people have to get out and stretch their wings. Through the years, I've worked with many young people. It's been my experience that most of them end up finding their way back to their roots. Maybe some of the youth from the area will make their way back here and revitalize the area. There are entire home improvement shows of people doing just that. They paint colorful murals on the sides of the buildings and attract tourists to the area. Peggy was always artistic. Maybe she could paint the murals."

She met Mr. Caldwell's eyes in the rearview mirror. His face had lost all color and his eyes were glassed over. "Are you feeling another attack?"

Landon leaned over and put the back of his hand on the man's forehead. "He feels cool." Placing his palms on either side of Mr. Caldwell's head, Landon turned him to face him. The older man mumbled and slumped against the seat.

"Mr. Caldwell. Wake up." Landon shook the man's limp body. "I don't think he can wait twenty minutes for something to increase his blood sugar. I'll call an ambulance. Pull over."

She spotted a road sign ahead. "I have a better idea. We're less than a mile from his home. Let's go there. If Peggy is home, she can assist us. If not, the house key is on his key chain. We can get him inside and get food in him more quickly. It takes a while for ambulances to reach people this far from the hospitals."

"He needs to be seen by a doctor. The way he's acting isn't normal." Landon pulled out his phone. "Do you know his address? I can have them meet us there."

Brooklyn frowned. "No. I don't remember it. Once we have him comfortable, we can call the ambulance. The address should be on the mailbox. If not, it will be on a bill or something inside the house."

Mr. Caldwell mumbled incoherently.

"Are you sure you remember how to get to his house?"

"Absolutely. He was the closest neighbor to Mrs. Jane's house. There might have been a third of a mile distance between them. Peggy and I walked back and forth through the pasture separating the houses all the time."

"Then step on it," Landon commanded.

She took the turn a little faster than she intended. The tires lost their grip and the back of the vehicle skidded. Something in the trunk slid and banged. Sounded bigger than a cane. She hoped it wasn't anything that could be damaged. Straightening the wheel, she regained control of the vehicle and sped over the bumpy potholes in the old country road.

Soon the cheerful yellow house with white shutters came into view. Other than faded paint that had peeled in a few spots and a yard that needed tending, it looked exactly as she remembered.

Pulling into the drive, she parked and quickly exited the vehicle to assist Landon, who had hopped out before she'd come to a stop. He already had Mr. Caldwell's door open and was helping him stand.

Leaning back into the vehicle, Brooklyn snatched the keys out of ignition and pressed the button to release the trunk. It rose with a beeping sound.

"Leave the cane. I have others in the house. That one stays in the car." Mr. Caldwell snatched the keys out of her hand and pressed the button to lower the trunk.

She had never witnessed her friend's father being so mean. Was grumpiness a symptom of low blood sugar?

"Here, let me take those." Brooklyn reached for the keys, but he held them out of her reach. "I just want the key to open the house door."

"I can do that." He huffed, pulled his arm free from Landon's grasp and shuffled the few feet to the porch steps. Grabbing the railing, he hauled himself up them. After fumbling with the keys for a minute, he inserted the correct one into the lock, twisted the knob and led them inside.

Brooklyn felt like she'd stepped back in time. Not a single thing had changed since the last time she'd crossed the threshold. Pictures of Peggy and her parents adorned the pale pink walls, and the same hunter green flower-print carpet runner ran the length of the stairs. And the scent of a roast cooking wafted in the air, reminding her of Sunday dinners with Mrs. Jane.

She looked up the stairs. "Is Peggy at work? Do we need to call her?"

"No." The elderly man missed a step and stumbled, breaking his fall by leaning onto the antique Queen Anne entry table. "She doesn't have her phone on her."

Brooklyn didn't know many adults who didn't have their personal phones on them, even at work. What kind of career had her friend chosen? Brooklyn could picture her being an art teacher or a lawyer.

Landon grasped Mr. Caldwell's upper arm and guided him to the sofa.

"I'll see what I can find in the kitchen that will bring up his sugar quickly." She crossed through the dining room and into the small galley kitchen.

A slow cooker sat on the countertop, a pot roast with carrots and potatoes simmering inside. Opening cabinets and drawers, she found a jar of peanut butter, then grabbed a tablespoon and headed back into the living room, opening the jar as she went.

Mr. Caldwell sat on the sofa with his head resting against the back and his eyes closed, while Landon hovered nearby.

"Here you go, Mr. Caldwell." Brooklyn dipped the spoon into the jar and scooped out a heaping helping of the smooth, brown goo.

He accepted the spoon and quickly licked it clean. Then he leaned back and closed his eyes. Was he okay? Did he need another serving?

She wrapped her fingers around the spoon, intent on

taking it and scooping out another helping for him. Mr. Caldwell's eyes flew open. She jumped back with a start. Placing her hand on her chest, she took several slow breaths, willing her racing heart to return to a normal, steady rate. "You startled me."

"Not my fault. You're the one who tried to steal my spoon." He glared at her.

Landon quickly inserted himself between the older man and Brooklyn. Ever her protector.

"It's okay." She patted his shoulder. "But maybe you should call the ambulance now. It would be good for a paramedic or doctor to check him out."

Mr. Caldwell pushed up off the couch faster than she would have expected of him. "I'm sorry. I didn't mean to sound snippety. I also don't need the expense of an ambulance ride or an ER visit." He shuffled around them and headed to the kitchen. "I'm already starting to feel better."

Brooklyn leaned in close to Landon. "I've never known him to say a cross word to anyone. I'm not sure what's going on with him," she whispered.

What had happened to the man who had been so loving and kind to her—a foster child without a father figure? Brooklyn prayed she'd have a chance to talk to Peggy and find out what was going on and if there was anything she could do to help.

"He seems less shaky than earlier," Landon observed as Mr. Caldwell ambled into the kitchen.

He'd never been around anyone with a sugar low before, so he didn't have a baseline for normal behavior. Even if he did, he knew every person reacted differently in a medical crisis. He couldn't worry about the older man right now, especially since he appeared to be fine. "We need to go. It's getting late. I don't think Mr. Caldwell needs to be out on the road again today. I'd hate to be responsible if he had another medical emergency and had a wreck, hurting himself or someone else. We're only twenty-five minutes from the sheriff's office. I'll call Heath. Maybe he can come get us."

Brooklyn nodded. "I agree. You call Heath, and I'll make sure Mr. Caldwell doesn't need anything. I want to give him my cell number so Peggy can contact me."

"Okay." He pulled out his phone and punched in Heath's number as she walked into the kitchen.

The phone rang once, then there was a beep followed by an automated voice telling him service was unavailable at this time. He hung up and tried again. Same response. The storms must have affected some of the cell towers. Now what?

Shoving his phone into his back pocket, he made his way through the dining room to the kitchen.

"I don't know why y'all are bothering the sheriff. I told you I'd drive you. And I will, after I've had something to eat." Mr. Caldwell lifted the lid on the slow cooker and inhaled deeply. "Mmm. At least let me feed you before you go?"

"That's nice of you to offer, but—" Brooklyn spotted him standing in the doorway. "Oh, Landon, is Heath on his way?"

"I couldn't get through. Seems like the storm may have taken out a tower."

Her brow furrowed. "But you talked to him earlier, right?"

"Yes, but my phone could be pinging off a different tower now." He rubbed the back of his neck and looked at the older man. "I hate to ask, but—"

"Of course, I'll drive you." Mr. Caldwell pulled a plate

out of the cabinet and spooned a serving of the roast into it. "First, we eat. Then, we go."

"That's—"

"Don't argue. I need to eat, and then I'll be fine to drive you," Mr. Caldwell declared. "And you two look like you haven't eaten in days. I'm simply trying to be hospitable. Just say thank you and eat. Then we'll take care of the rest of our business."

"Yes, sir." Landon smiled. The older man was astute. It hadn't been days since they'd last eaten, but it had been over thirty hours since they'd had a full meal. If food would enable Mr. Caldwell to regain his strength enough to drive them the rest of the way to Barton Creek, delaying their journey long enough to eat couldn't hurt, could it? "Thank you."

"You two go have a seat at the dining table. I'll bring everything out." Mr. Caldwell jerked his head toward the doorway that led into the dining room and reached into the cabinet for another plate.

"Oh, no. We can't do that." Brooklyn picked up the plate full of roast he'd sat on the countertop.

He sighed and dropped the serving spoon onto a ceramic spoon rest. "You two young people are making me feel like a helpless old man. I promise you I am more than capable of taking care of myself. Now, get out of here and let me be the host in my home."

"But—"

"I can roll everything into the dining room." He raised his hand, pointing the empty plate at a small two-tier rolling cart.

"Okay." She nodded, placed the plate onto the cart and walked out of the room, passing Landon without saying a word.

He met Mr. Caldwell's eyes. The older man looked away and started filling the plate in his hand. Landon knew, as he aged, he'd want to remain as independent as possible and wouldn't want anyone hovering over him, but he prayed he would never make anyone feel small for offering a helping hand. Mr. Caldwell shuffled over to the cart and placed the second plate beside the first. After a quick glance his way, Mr. Caldwell continued with his task at hand.

Landon turned toward the dining room, surprised to find that Brooklyn wasn't there. He made his way to the living room and found her standing in front of a wall of photographs.

"I'm guessing that's Peggy." He pointed at the photo of a young girl with bright blue eyes, dressed in overalls, with her brown hair in pigtails. She was in a field and was peeking around one of the big, round hay bales scattered about.

"I remember that day as if it were yesterday," Brooklyn replied. "They had just finished baling the hay and Peggy wanted to play hide-and-go-seek."

"Doesn't look like there would be many places to hide out in an open field like that."

She laughed. "It wasn't so much about hiding as it was about not getting caught. The one hiding would run as fast as they could once the seeker started counting. Then they'd slip behind a bale and listen. As long as the seeker didn't guess which bale the hider had chosen as their *first* hiding spot, they would be safe."

"Since the bales were large, when the seeker would go behind one, the one hiding would move spots," he surmised.

"Exactly."

"Too bad the person taking the photo didn't capture you in the picture, too. I'd love to see what you looked like as a child."

"I was. In the photo. Or, at least the original copy that used to hang here." She pointed at something in the corner of the photo. Although her lips lifted, her smile didn't reach her eyes. "This is the tip of my tennis shoe. I guess someone cut me out of the picture after I moved to another home and we lost contact."

Landon scrutinized the photo. Why would someone alter the memory of children enjoying a game together? Mr. Caldwell had seemed happy to see Brooklyn—Hope—again, after all these years. Would Peggy feel the same way about a reunion with her childhood friend?

"Dinner is served." Mr. Caldwell stood in the dining room next to the table.

To put a smile on her face, Landon turned to Brooklyn and offered her his arm. "May I escort you to the dining room?"

She giggled and slipped her hand into the crook of his elbow. "Thank you, sir."

Mr. Caldwell shook his head and settled into his seat at one end of the oblong table. Landon escorted Brooklyn to the right side of the table, where Mr. Caldwell had placed plates with heaping helpings of roast, carrots and potatoes, along with rolls and drinks—glasses of iced tea for his guests and water for himself—in front of three chairs, the one he sat in and the ones on either side of him. Landon pulled out the chair on Mr. Caldwell's left for Brooklyn. Once she was seated, he moved to the chair on the other side of the table, across from her.

Mr. Caldwell forked a baby carrot and shoved it into his mouth.

Landon and Brooklyn exchanged glances.

"What's wrong?" Mr. Caldwell demanded after swallowing his food.

"Well, sir..." Landon crossed his hands and placed them on the edge of the table in front of him. "Aren't we going to say grace?"

Their host dropped his fork, and it clattered onto his plate. "I don't *pray*...anymore. One day, you may realize, like I did, that God doesn't care about you as much as you do him."

"I believe you have that wrong, sir. God does care about us." He reached across the table and clasped Brooklyn's hand. "And He has protected us. Multiple times. We could have died..." *Don't share more than necessary.* "In the tornado or when my brakes failed. But we didn't. And now we're here, and Br—Hope has gotten to see you and will now have a chance to reconnect with Peggy."

"You make a good point. Would you say grace? After you thank God for the food, thank Him for allowing our paths to cross." Mr. Caldwell smiled, folded his hands and bowed his head.

Landon couldn't tell if the elderly man was being sincere or if he was making fun of his faith. Brooklyn squeezed his hand. He bowed his head and prayed. "Our kind and most holy Heavenly Father, thank You for the food that has been placed before us. We pray it will be nourishing to our bodies. We especially thank You for watching over us today and protecting us from harm, and for Mr. Caldwell and his hospitality. We pray You guide our steps as we strive to be a light unto the world. Amen."

FOURTEEN

Amen. Brooklyn silently echoed Landon's prayer. A clock chimed the hour. She looked over her shoulder at the antique grandfather clock in the corner of the dining room. Five o'clock. She had always loved the sound of that clock chiming the hour. "What time will Peggy be home?"

"Don't worry about Peggy." Mr. Caldwell shoved another bite of food into his mouth, chewed and swallowed. Then he pointed the handle of his fork at her plate. "You'll see Peggy soon. I promise. And I'm sure she's been anxiously awaiting your return."

Wrapping her hand around her glass, she picked it up and took a long drink. The cold, sweet liquid ran down her parched throat. Placing the glass back onto the table, she picked up the fork and took a bite of her food, glancing at Landon. He was devouring the food on his plate. It was no surprise. He had to be starving. He'd done most of the work yesterday, getting them downriver, protecting them from the storm and guiding them out of the woods and back to the cabin.

Brooklyn swallowed the roast. She hadn't even realized how hungry she was. Her stomach growled, and she took another bite of food. The roast was delicious.

"Thank you for the meal. It's been a long time since I've

had a true home-cooked meal." She smiled at Mr. Caldwell. "I mean, I cook at home. But living alone, I don't make what you would call traditional home-cooked family meals— roasts, meat loaf, chicken and dumplings, things like that. I've missed them."

"I'm glad you could share this meal with me." He took a sip of his water, and a wistful expression crossed his eyes. "I cook meals like this all the time. Habit, I guess. The thing I miss is having family to share it with."

"But you have Peggy. You said she lives with you, right?"

"Peggy just *sleeps* here. That's all."

Brooklyn frowned. How could her friend be so thoughtless? The young girl she'd known wouldn't treat an elderly parent with disrespect. Peggy had always been close to both her parents. Had her mom leaving them changed her?

Landon cleared his throat. "Tell me about Brooklyn as a child?"

"Who's Brooklyn?" Mr. Caldwell looked from Landon to her and back again.

"I'm Brooklyn," she breathed.

"No, you're Hope Jennings."

"Not any longer. Now, I'm Brooklyn Thomas."

"Why would you change your name? Are you hiding from someone? The law?"

Hiding from someone...yes. But he found me anyway.

"Nothing like that. My name has always been Brooklyn. I just preferred to go by Hope when I was younger." Brooklyn smiled. "I promise, I'm not running from the law or. Believe it or not, I actually have a college degree, which provides me with a steady job and a home of my own."

"Well, good for you." He took a bite of his roll, then snickered. "I guess people can turn their lives around. I fully expected you to die of a drug overdose at a young age."

She gasped. "Why would you say that?"

Although she would never admit it to the Mr. Caldwell, she had come close to doing just that, twice, before she escaped Nikki and her boyfriend's control.

"Because, when you were eleven years old, you brought over a pack of cigarettes—a gateway drug—and convinced my Peggy it would be a good idea to smoke them."

The memory of the last Saturday Brooklyn and Peggy spent together played through her mind like an old movie. On Friday Mrs. Jane had taken the girls to the Corner Quick Stop after school, and the older girl had tried to convince Brooklyn to steal cigarettes so Peggy could teach her how to smoke. Brooklyn had been afraid of being caught and never being allowed to go back to the convenience store, so she had refused. The next day a repairman had come to Mrs. Jane's house to fix the dishwasher. Mrs. Jane had given Brooklyn permission to go play at Peggy's for an hour. On her way out the door, she had seen an open pack of cigarettes in the repairman's toolbox. She had swiped them and slipped them into her pocket. Then she'd taken the lighter Mrs. Jane kept on the mantel in the living room for lighting the fire, banged out the door and run as fast as she could, afraid of being caught.

Arriving at the Caldwell farm, she'd asked Peggy if they could play outside. Once she got her friend out of earshot of her parents, she'd shown her the cigarettes and lighter. They had giggled and gone into the barn, climbing into the hayloft, and Brooklyn had smoked for the first—and last—time.

Brooklyn had coughed, puffed and choked her way through half of one cigarette. Then she'd vomited while

Peggy had leaned against the barn wall, puffing smoke rings and laughing at her. Mr. Caldwell might have thought Brooklyn introduced Peggy to cigarettes, but her friend's older cousin Chad had already taught her the bad habit and the fine art of puffing smoke rings. Mr. Caldwell had caught them and had called Mrs. Jane to come get her.

Brooklyn had apologized profusely to her foster mom, but Mrs. Jane had just looked at her with disappointment in her eyes and shaken her head. The next day, Mrs. Jane had a heart attack, and Brooklyn had been immediately transferred to another foster home.

They continued to eat in silence until they'd all cleaned their plates. Her mouth was dry. She picked up her glass of tea and drank it all in one gulp. Mr. Caldwell quickly refilled her glass, along with Landon's. Then he used his roll to sop up the remaining roast juice on his plate, ate it and refilled his own glass with ice water.

"You're not having tea? I remember sweet tea used to be your favorite," Brooklyn observed.

He took a sip of water. "Sadly, my doctor advised me to cut back on a few things, and sweet tea was one thing I had to give up. Never could make myself drink unsweet tea."

That made sense, she guessed. Though he'd always said, no matter what situation he found himself in healthwise as he aged, he'd never give up his sweet tea.

An overwhelming heat engulfed her, as if someone had turned on a furnace inside her body. Perspiration broke out along the hairline at the base of her neck. She gathered her hair with one hand and held it off her neck, fanning herself. What was going on? Brooklyn couldn't remember ever feeling so clammy. Had she caught a cold from the river and rain yesterday?

"You're looking pale. Are you okay?" Landon pushed

back his chair, stood and stumbled, falling back onto the seat. "Whoa."

"I'm okay." She narrowed her eyes, trying to get him to come into focus. "Are you okay?"

"Yeah, I just need to sit a minute."

Mr. Caldwell stood and started gathering dishes off the table. "You two just sit here and relax. I'll clear the table and load the dishwasher."

Her head spun and her stomach felt queasy. The sound of Mr. Caldwell whistling in the kitchen and dishes clanking as he loaded them into the dishwasher echoed in the small space. If he were well enough to clean up, then it couldn't be food poisoning.

Pressing down on the table, she pushed to her feet. Her chair fell to the hardwood floor with a thud. Holding on to the table, she inched her way toward the entry hall.

"Where are you going?" Landon asked, his voice barely above a whisper.

"Restroom."

He shoved to his feet. Reaching her side in two unsteady steps, he grasped her arm. "We need to get out of here. I feel…" His eyes closed, and then he reopened them, stretching them wide. "Something isn't right."

She knew he was trying to tell her something important, but his words tumbled around inside her head, not penetrating her brain. The room tilted, and nausea bubbled inside her.

"I'm going to…throw up." She covered her mouth with her hand, broke free of his grasp and stumbled down the hall, using the wall to keep herself upright.

She pushed open the bathroom door, rushing inside and closing it behind her. Then she sank onto the floor in front of the toilet. Ten minutes later, she lay on the cool tile floor, weak and clammy, but the nauseous feeling had passed and the room no longer spun. *Dear Lord, whatever this bug is, please let this pass quickly.*

Grasping the cabinet, she pulled herself to her feet, leaned over the sink and splashed cold water on her face. She needed to check on Landon. What had he been trying to tell her earlier?

Leaving the bathroom, she made her way down the hall and into the living room. Where were Mr. Caldwell and Landon? She checked the dining room and kitchen, but the men were nowhere to be found. Had they gone outside?

Brooklyn stepped onto the front porch. "Landon! Mr. Caldwell!" Stumbling, she made her way down the steps. "Where are you?"

She heard a scraping sound. Looking around, the barn caught her attention, and she started across the lawn toward it. "Landon!"

The barn door slid open and Mr. Caldwell stepped out, closing it behind him and clicking a padlock into place. He made his way to her, moving faster than she'd seen him move all afternoon, one foot dragging slightly. "Are you feeling better? I wish you wouldn't have been sick."

Heat crept up her neck. Had Landon heard her vomiting, too? She'd forgotten how thin the walls were in the Caldwells' old farmhouse. "Where's Landon? I can't find him anywhere."

"Oh…uh…" He looked around. "I think he said something about walking up the road to see if he could get a better signal on his cell phone."

That didn't sound like Landon. He hadn't left her side once since Chastiser set her house on fire.

"Let me grab my keys and get you some ginger tea to settle your stomach, and we'll go search for him." Mr.

Caldwell grasped her elbow and guided her to his car, settling her into the front passenger seat. "Wait here."

An uneasy feeling that had nothing to do with nausea settled over her. She rubbed her temples, desperate to keep her nerves at bay. Brooklyn needed to remain focused and find Landon, quickly. For the first time since leaving the hospital, she felt alone. Which intensified her vulnerability.

"Uh...wha..." Landon licked his parched lips. Why was his mouth so dry? And what was the strange taste in the back of his throat? "Ow..." His head throbbed as a sharp pain ran along the top of his skull.

It felt like his head was going to split in two. Seeking to hold the sides of his head to prevent such an unthinkable thing, he lifted his arms. But something held them at his sides.

He blinked several times, forcing his eyes wide. Everything in front of him was blurry. He looked down. He was on a dirt floor. His wrists were zip-tied—one to a pole and the other to a metal gate. Looking around, he took in his surroundings. He was in a barn, but how had he gotten here? And who had tied him up?

The last thing he remembered was Brooklyn going into the bathroom saying she was going to be sick. *Then what happened? Think!*

Why was his brain so fuzzy? *I've been drugged!*

He fought against the restraints, the bindings cutting into his wrists. Several minutes later, he slumped against the wooden wall behind his back, exhausted. His wrists were bloody, and his muscles ached. Worst of all, his actions had been futile.

Taking a deep breath, he released it slowly, willing his heart rate to slow so it wouldn't feel like it was going to beat out of his chest. He wouldn't do Brooklyn any good if he couldn't get free.

"Come on. Use your brain. Think through your next steps. Don't waste your energy acting recklessly," he chided himself.

Closing his eyes, he worked to clear the cobwebs from his brain, recalling his last memory.

After Brooklyn had gone into the bathroom, Mr. Caldwell came out of the kitchen and asked to talk to Landon in private. They went outside. Landon stumbled going down the steps, and Mr. Caldwell had grasped Landon's upper arm.

Landon gasped. The memory of what happened next rushed to the forefront of his mind like a tsunami.

Mr. Caldwell had guided him to the barn, telling Landon he knew who was after Brooklyn. Except that neither he nor Brooklyn had mentioned anything to Mr. Caldwell about anyone being after Brooklyn. Landon had turned to confront the older man. Mr. Caldwell had smirked and let go of his arm. Then Landon had lost his balance and fallen onto the dirt floor. He hadn't understood what was wrong with his body. Why his legs were unwilling to hold him up. When he had looked up at the older man, Mr. Caldwell was wearing the evilest smile Landon had ever seen.

The elderly man had gleefully declared that he was Chastiser and it was time for Brooklyn to receive her punishment and be sent to her place of eternal doom. Then Mr. Caldwell had crossed to a wall of tools and run his hand over the sharp instruments, as if trying to determine which one to use to dismember Landon.

That's when Brooklyn had called their names from the yard. He'd tried to yell for her to run, but the words came out as a whisper. And Chastiser had picked up a shovel and smashed it against the side of Landon's head.

That was the last thing he remembered. Until now.

What time was it? Dark shadows had settled around him. It had to be getting late? Would Heath or Jackson come looking for them? He'd told Heath the name of the person driving them. But he couldn't depend on anyone to reach them in time to save Brooklyn.

"Ugh!" He had to get free! Landon struggled against his restraints, and the metal gate clanked.

He eyed the gate. For the first time since he'd regained consciousness, he really examined it. It was old and rusty. But the part that interested him the most was the rails. Rusted metal slats. And the rust had caused the edges to become jagged.

Making a fist, he puffed out a breath and drew his elbow to his side then punched outward. The zip tie skidded back and forth across the metal as the rusty edges slowly sawed into the thick plastic. Fifty or so repetitions later, the plastic broke and his left arm was free. "Yes!"

Grasping the wooden pole that still held his right arm captive, he pulled himself to his feet. Rolling his shoulders and stomping his feet, he worked to regain circulation in his limbs. Then he examined the pole. It was smooth. There wasn't a knot or nail anywhere on it. He could not saw the remaining zip tie off his wrist as he had the other one. He tried to push the tail of the zip tie back through the head, but it would not budge. Now what?

Landon patted his pockets and smiled. He pulled his phone out. "I guess he forgot to check my pockets in his hurry to get away," he said aloud to the empty barn.

He tapped the screen. It remained black. He pressed the power button. Nothing. No! This could not be happening.

The barn door rattled. He froze. Was Chastiser back? If so, did it mean he'd already killed Brooklyn? *Please, Lord, no! Please, let her still be alive. Let me get to her in time. Don't let me fail her.*

The rattling grew louder. Landon put his free hand over the zip tie and pushed it down the pole until he was back to his seated position. He wasn't sure how he'd overtake Chastiser and get free, but he wouldn't stand a chance unless he could lull the killer into thinking he was still unconscious. Shoving his cell phone back into his pocket, he lifted his arm and held it against the metal gate, praying Chastiser wouldn't notice the zip tie was missing. Then he lowered his head and closed his eyes just as the door slid open.

The sound of footsteps rushed toward him. As they drew near, he dropped his hand, grabbed a handful of dirt and slung it at his attacker.

"Hey! Watch it!"

Landon's head jerked upward at the sound of Heath's voice. The sheriff towered over him, dusting dirt out of his hair. Jackson Knight walked around Heath, pulled a folding knife out of his pocket, flipped it open and cut the zip tie off Landon's right wrist, then gave him a hand up.

"I'm so glad you guys are here. We've got to find Brooklyn. Joseph Caldwell is Chastiser," Landon declared.

"We know," Jackson said. "The lab lifted a print off an unburned corner of the wooden box Tiffany's body was in. The print belonged to Caldwell."

"Well, come on. What are you waiting for? Let's go get him." Landon started for the door.

"He's not here." Heath put a hand on his arm, halting him. "The house is empty, and his car is gone. We had hoped it was stashed in here, which would mean he hadn't gone far, but…"

"Brooklyn?" His chest tightened, even though he already knew the answer.

"She's missing, too," Heath verified. "There's a shed on the other side of the house. We found a black truck inside. There was a wooden coffin in the truck bed."

"Since he left that here, it means he has another plan for killing her." Landon pulled his cell phone out of his pocket and held it up. "Whose vehicle did you drive? Do you have a phone charger that will work with my phone?"

"We're in mine," Heath said. "And yes, I do. Why?"

"We can track them. Brooklyn allowed me to put a location sharing app on her devices, including her smart watch. As long as she is still wearing it, we'll be able to find her. I just need to plug my phone in and let it charge a few minutes."

"What are we waiting for? Let's go," Jackson said.

The three men raced out of the barn and across the yard to Heath's SUV. Landon prayed the killer had overlooked Brooklyn's watch the same way he had his cell phone.

FIFTEEN

"Wake up," a male's voice whispered in her ear as someone tapped her cheek.

"You don't want to miss this. Come on, I didn't give you
that much Xyrem… Now, wake up!" he yelled.

She didn't want to wake up. She wanted to sleep. Her
head ached, and her eyelids felt like lead weights that
wouldn't budge. A floorboard creaked as the heavy thud
of footsteps echoed in the room.

"I'm beginning to think you're faking being asleep."
The man's voice grew angrier with each word. Who was
he? Why was he yelling at her? And where was Landon?
She needed Landon.

The scent of gasoline penetrated her brain, and her eyelids flew open. The shadow of a man, pouring fuel down
the center aisle of the room, greeted her.

"Chastiser." The word ripped from her throat.

The man laughed, a deep rumbling laughter. "And here
I was afraid you didn't recognize me."

"Mr. Caldwell?" She narrowed her eyes, her brow fur-
rowing. "What are—"

The reality of her situation jolted her fully alert. She was
tied to something heavy, her arms pressed to her sides, un-
able to move. Brooklyn twisted her neck and looked over

her shoulder. A wooden podium. She glanced around the room. Where was she? The center aisle led to a foyer where there was a double wooden door with a transom window above it. Wooden pews sat in neat rows on either side of the aisle, facing her. "Is this a church?"

"Of course. Where else would a sinner go for repentance?"

Tears welled up inside her. As much as she wished she could control her emotions and keep them at bay, fighting them would be impossible. They flowed freely down her face as quiet sobs racked her body.

Mr. Caldwell paused and looked at her. "I'm glad to see you're feeling remorseful. I guess you've realized your sins have caught up with you, huh? Well, it's too little, too late. It's time for your eternal punishment."

"What did I ever do to you? Why are you doing this?"

"What did you do?" He lifted the red gasoline container he held in his hands and doused the pew closest to him. "You came into our lives and filled our daughter's head with nonsense. Introduced her to cigarettes. Talked about what life was like with your mother—a drunkard, no less— and how you didn't have a bedtime or any chores, making it seem glamorous that she didn't care about you and you could do whatever you wanted. No rules! Or consequences!" He splashed gas up the aisle. "Because of your influence, Peggy started experimenting with alcohol and drugs. She died of an overdose on her eighteenth birthday."

Brooklyn's eyes widened. *"Peggy only sleeps here."*

Tears stung the backs of her eyes. She'd seen an urn on the mantel earlier, but hadn't wanted to pry, so she hadn't asked whose ashes were inside it, thinking it was probably one of Mr. Caldwell's parents.

"Her mom blamed me for being too strict," he continued

ranting. "Said I pushed her away, and I believed it. Until I saw you through the truck stop window. Then I knew the truth. The path Peggy took wasn't *my* fault. It was *yours*."

None of this made sense. Had he hated her for twenty-one years for smoking a cigarette in his barn with his daughter? What about the other women he had murdered? What *crimes* had they committed against him?

"I know you won't believe me, but Peggy is the one who dared me to steal cigarettes from the convenience store. She said her cousin Chad had taught her how to smoke. Said she'd teach me how to puff smoke rings if I got us some cigarettes."

"You didn't steal those cigarettes from the convenience store. You stole them from Mr. Davidson's toolbox. Peggy told me so."

"You're right. I did. I couldn't make myself steal from the convenience store. I was afraid if I got caught, Mrs. Jane wouldn't take me back there again and get me a snack after school. Mr. Davidson left his toolbox out. I saw half a pack of cigarettes and took them." The guilt that always assailed her when she thought of that last evening with Mrs. Jane welled up inside her. The disappointment in the older woman's eyes.

Focus! She pushed aside her emotions. If she wanted to live, she had to keep Mr. Caldwell talking, to prolong him from starting the fire and give Landon time to rescue her.

Where was Landon? Had Mr. Caldwell hurt him?

Lord, thanks to Lillian's teaching, if it's my time to die, I'm prepared. But please, don't let Landon lose his life because of me.

Mr. Caldwell had reached the middle of the room. She had to slow his progress. "Let's say you're right. Peggy's downfall was my fault and I deserve what you're doing to me. Why did you kill the other women? What was it… seven women? All murdered over the course of four years?"

His head snapped upward. "Judged and punished. Not murdered."

"What gave you the right to be their judge?" She could not control the rage building inside her. "Why not try to teach them about God's love and His forgiveness? Help them better their lives? It's what Landon and I are doing with the Lillian's Legacy Foundation."

"Yeah, I saw you on the television talking about it. But, again, it's *too little, too late* on your part." He emptied the last of the gasoline and tossed the plastic can in the corner. "As for my being the judge and jury for the other women's crimes, I tried talking to the first woman, but she wouldn't even sit down with me. I realized I was wasting my breath. There wasn't anything left to do. I wasn't able to save my child—or my marriage after the heartache Peggy put us through—so I figured I would do the heroic thing and end other parents' suffering."

"How is that ending the parents' suffering? You murdered their daughters. That increased their suffering!" He made absolutely no sense.

"At least they could tell their friends someone murdered their daughter. They wouldn't have to admit that she died of a drug overdose because she turned her back on them and rejected the morals they'd tried to instill in her."

Understanding why a person would kill had never been something Brooklyn could do. No matter how hard she tried, she couldn't fathom any reason that would make someone take the life of another human being. Even having this conversation with the serial killer in front of her, she still could not comprehend his rationale. Pure evil. That's all it was.

The conversation was making her repulsed, but she had to keep him talking. "The FBI never found a connection between the women you mur—" *Angering him will cause him to clam up. And he'll be in a bigger hurry to kill you. Choose your words carefully.* "The women you *judged*. Were they friends of Peggy's?"

"No. They were women who just crossed my path. Much the same way you did, when I saw you waiting tables at the truck stop." He shook his head and started sloshing more gasoline around the room. "I may not have known their names before they died, but I knew what they were like…their selfish, addiction obsessed personalities…the same as Peggy."

"You said Peggy died on her eighteenth birthday. That would have been the eleventh of August. The body of the first woman you killed was found September first. Three weeks later. You didn't waste any time, did you?"

"Impressive. I'm honored that you've kept up with my stats."

"Lillian wanted me to remember what I had escaped. She said it would make me stronger."

"Lillian? The one your foundation is named after. Is she the FBI agent who stopped your trip to the afterlife last time? I saw the FBI director's interview on the news after you escaped the first time. It disappointed me he didn't mention you—or the agent who rescued you—by name." He laughed. "Won't Lillian be sad to know that it was just a delayed departure and your ticket wasn't canceled?"

"Fortunately, she won't know about your recent actions. She passed away a year ago."

"Well, then, maybe she'll be waiting on the other side to greet you. That is assuming she's in the place you're headed."

Love filled Brooklyn's heart. She knew Lillian would greet her in Heaven. The warmhearted, loving woman had treated Brooklyn as her own daughter. She had taught her about God's love and forgiveness. Lillian was the reason she was a Christian. Some of Brooklyn's fondest memories were the Bible studies with Lillian at her kitchen table.

Even though Brooklyn knew where she'd spend eternity—it would not be where Mr. Caldwell hoped to send her—and she no longer feared death, she wasn't ready to leave this life yet. She had so many things she wanted to do.

Memories of Landon from the past few days flashed through her mind...holding her hand, hugging her, watching movies, teaching her to canoe, covering her during the storm, protecting her... She didn't want their time together to end. Realization dawned. Her breath caught and her heart skipped a beat. Brooklyn loved Landon. For the first time in her adult life, she could see herself getting married and raising a family. Together, they could break their dysfunctional families' cycles. They could build a beautiful life together. But the only way that would happen would be if she could keep the killer intent on taking her life talking and give Landon time to rescue her once more.

"They're in the national park!" Landon zoomed in on the map. "They entered the park at the Townsend entrance and turned right. There haven't been any updates on the tracking app since then. That was...forty-five minutes ago." Landon's chest tightened.

"You don't think... Could he have..." He swallowed. "Taken her there to dispose of her body."

"Don't let your mind go there, Landon," Heath advised, activating his lights and siren. "Most likely, they drove out of cell service range. We're five minutes from Townsend. Hold on to positive thoughts. And pray."

Lord, give me strength. Help me not give in to my fears, and above all else, please keep Brooklyn safe.

"Caldwell is a former park ranger." Jackson spoke up from the back seat. "He knows his way around. He won't risk starting a fire where there's a lot of through traffic. I expect he's headed to a remote area."

"Well, that's not really reassuring." Landon shifted in his seat and looked at the agent. "Are you suggesting he'd take her into the wilderness? That doesn't track with his MO. He leaves his victims where someone will find them…usually within a day or less. I've always thought he did it that way, along with leaving Scripture, because he was trying to send a message to the world."

"I agree." Jackson tapped his cell's screen and pulled up the keypad, punched in a number and lifted his phone to his ear. "This is Agent Knight. I need an agent to meet me at the Cades Cove entrance…yes, I realize that area was closed off at sundown. It's possible the serial killer Chastiser is holding an abducted woman there."

Jackson listened to the person on the other end of the line.

"No. Wait for me. We don't want anyone alerting him we're coming."

More silence as Jackson listened again. Landon itched to reach back, take the phone and put it on speaker. Instead, he balled his hand into a fist and concentrated on his breathing.

"That's a good idea. Fly high enough he can't hear it or see it easily. Also, try to get an ATV out there, in case we have to go deeper into the woods." He pulled the phone away from his ear and placed it on speaker. "Sheriff Dalton, what's our ETA?"

"Twenty-five minutes or less, depending on traffic."

"Did you hear that?"

"Yes, sir," came the reply. "I'll have everything ready and waiting for you."

Jackson disconnected the call, then met Landon's gaze.

"What makes you think he has Brooklyn inside Cades Cove?"

"As you pointed out, Chastiser has a distinct MO. It's highly unlikely he drove into the park with a wooden box strapped to his car. Plus, Brooklyn escaped the last time he tried to kill her that way. So, it's doubtful he'll try that again. But he will want someone to find his latest victim as soon as possible. The gates into Cades Cove are closed at sundown. Being a former park ranger, he knows trails and roads in there where he could hide until everyone was out of the area."

"What if you're wrong? Aren't there other places in the park that are closed after dark?"

"Chastiser's murders have a religious theme. All the profilers who have studied his slayings agree he is acting as judge, jury and executioner of women he deems to be sinners. If he can't burn his victim—"

"Brooklyn." Landon closed his eyes, took a deep breath and opened them again. "Please, use her name. I don't want to consider her a victim."

Jackson typed something into his cell phone, then lifted his eyes slightly above Landon's head. Landon turned to see the agent and the sheriff exchange a glance in the rearview mirror. He knew he sounded ridiculous. Technically, she was a victim. A killer had targeted and tracked her, but if Landon thought of her in those terms, it would be harder to hold out hope that she was still alive.

"If he can't burn Brooklyn in a wooden casket, he will

look for a suitable replacement option. I believe," Jackson said, "Chastiser has taken Brooklyn to Cades Cove because there are three old church buildings in that area—which ties into his theme. If he sets one of the churches on fire, especially after dark in an area that's closed to the public, it would take a while for anyone to notice the smoke and respond to put it out."

The agent's logic was sound. Landon prayed he was right. "When you were talking to your agent, you said, 'Fly high enough he can't hear it or see it easily.' Were you talking about a helicopter?"

"No. A drone. If my guy spots suspicious activity at a specific church, we go straight to that building, saving time."

"Isn't the loop eleven miles long? And a one-way road?" Landon tried to remember where the churches were along the loop, but he hadn't visited the national park in more than twenty years.

"Actually, there are two lanes—Sparks Lane and Hyatt Lane—that connect both sides of the loop. But all three of the old church buildings are on the upper end of the loop, within the first three miles."

Landon turned back around and focused on the road ahead. They had entered the park and were driving along the winding roads that led to Cades Cove.

Mr. Caldwell, with his injured leg and friendly nature, had fooled him just like his dad had all those times he'd promised Landon he would become a better husband and father. Red-hot anger at himself rose in him.

Lord, I failed to protect my mom and now I've failed Brooklyn. Why do I always fail the women I love?

Love? No wonder Heath and Jackson had shared that look earlier. They must have realized his feelings even before he was willing to admit them to himself. *I do. I love her, Lord. Please, don't take her away from me. Give me a chance to make this up to her and show her I can be the life partner that she deserves. If she will have me, I promise to love her with all my heart and protect her with my life.*

Jackson's phone rang, and Landon twisted in his seat once again.

"Yes...okay...that's good... We're—" He sighed and put his phone in his pocket. "I lost the connection. But the good news is the drone operator detected movement at the third church on the loop."

"Did he see Brooklyn?" Hope and dread collided inside Landon's chest.

"He did. She's tied up, and Caldwell is still inside the church with her."

"We're here," Heath declared.

Landon looked around as they drove through the open gate, a park ranger closing it behind them as a man wearing an FBI tactical vest jogged over to their vehicle.

Heath stopped and rolled down the back seat window.

"Hop in," Jackson ordered before the officer could speak.

The agent did as commanded, and as soon as his door closed, Heath took off again, guiding their vehicle along the narrow, curvy road at a max speed of thirty miles per hour, ten miles above the posted limit.

"Agent Hawkins, you have less than five minutes to fill us in," Jackson said.

"Agent Barrett is waiting on us, with Ranger Payne, about two-tenths of a mile from the church. We're using two-way radios to stay in communication." Agent Hawkins held up a small handheld device.

"How did they get so close undetected?" Heath asked.

"Horses from the Cades Cove Riding Stables," Agent

Hawkins replied. "Barrett and Payne are using the drone and binoculars to keep a visual on the suspect."

"What can you tell us about the situation? Does Brooklyn appear to be unharmed?" Landon asked. He knew he should let Jackson take charge of the conversation since he was the officer in charge, but he couldn't help himself.

"She's alert. And seems to be having a conversation with the perp. According to Agent Barrett, she's spunky. Apparently, whatever she's saying has been making the man with her angry. Which is either brave or reckless, considering he has a gas can and is getting ready to set fire to the building."

"Have you alerted the fire and rescue unit?" Jackson asked.

"Yes, sir. They're on their way with the tanker truck. An ambulance also has been dispatched. I've instructed both units not to run sirens or lights. They should enter the cove any minute now. I told them not to get any closer than a mile and wait for our instructions."

"Sounds like you've taken care of everything."

Landon appreciated the agent's actions to protect the church building that had been constructed more than one hundred years ago, but he was more concerned with protecting the woman inside it. He prayed Caldwell didn't hear them coming and hurt Brooklyn before he could get her out of the building.

Two horses, standing twenty feet off the road with their reins tied to trees, came into view. Heath slowed his SUV and pulled off the pavement on the left side of the narrow, one-lane road. Landon released a breath, grasped the door handle and bolted from the vehicle. Whatever it took, he would get to Brooklyn before Chastiser could harm her.

SIXTEEN

Mr. Caldwell... No. She had to stop thinking of him as Mr. Caldwell. Mr. Caldwell had been the father of her childhood friend. He'd bought her ice cream and taken her on the roller coaster at the fair. The man who stood before her was not the same one she'd known. This man was Chastiser. A killer. And he hadn't just killed once, but seven times. Before Lillian retired from the FBI, she had brought home the files on every one of Chastiser's victims, trying to find something that linked them and connected them to Brooklyn. The only things they'd had in common were their ages—ranging from late teens to early twenties—drug addiction and being homeless. Some, like Brooklyn, had been unwillingly trafficked. But even having those things in common, Brooklyn had escaped that lifestyle and had been working to get back on her feet, with dreams of earning her GED and going to night school, before Chastiser had abducted her the first time. So even that link between her and the others hadn't been a solid one. Until now.

"Catching up with you has been... I want to say interesting, but it hasn't been. So, I'm done with the chitchat. I need to get back home and deal with your pesky private investigator friend. I would have preferred killing him before I brought you out here, but you interrupted my plans," Chastiser said, pulling her from her thoughts.

Landon is still alive. Thank You, Lord! She lifted her chin, meeting Chastiser's eyes. "I would say I'm sorry for interrupting your plans...but I'm not."

A sneer curled his lips. "Since you're in a building and not an enclosed casket, maybe you'll be more fortunate than the others and the smoke inhalation will kill you before the actual fire reaches you. I can't risk being caught in the fire—I poured a circle of fuel around the building so I can be outside when I ignite it. Enjoy watching the flames as they grow bigger and work their way toward you."

Brooklyn swallowed the gasp that threatened to escape, refusing to give him the satisfaction of knowing his words had bothered her. Breaking eye contact, she looked out the window that overlooked the graveyard. A full moon had risen above the tombstones dating back a hundred years or more. Hardworking people who'd lived in the remote area, raising families and growing crops. Strong people who were not afraid to face the uncertainty of mountain life in the eighteen hundreds. Movement in the tree line bordering the cemetery caught her attention. Was someone out there in the shadows? Or was the wind swaying the trees? She looked at the maple tree closest to the window. It stood perfectly still.

Hope surged in her. It had to be Landon. He'd come to save her. She had to keep Chastiser talking just a little longer and give Landon time to reach her.

"Selina Pounder." She turned her head forward. Facing the aisle, she watched as he walked away from her. "Beth NeSmith. Miranda Quimby," she said, getting louder with each name. "Kayleigh Lincoln. Summer Vanderford—"

"What are you doing?" Spinning around, he stumbled and caught the arm of a nearby pew to keep himself upright.

A peace she could never explain enveloped her. "I'm speaking the names of the women you murdered in cold blood," she replied, locking gazes with him and refusing to look away.

"Whatever makes you happy." He shrugged and turned back toward the door.

"Tiffany Carmichael!" she yelled at his retreating back.

Grasping the doorknob, he twisted sideways and glared at her. "Who?"

Tears stung the backs of her eyes. "Tiffany Carmichael. Your last victim. The one you killed to send a message to me."

Deep laughter rang out. The same amused laughter she'd heard many times when he would tell her and Peggy funny dad jokes or when they watched a comedy on television. His sheer joy at her anguish made her physically ill.

"Tiffany Carmichael. I didn't even know her name." He chuckled, shook his head, dug into his pocket and removed a box of matches. Removing a match, he closed the box and smiled at her.

"When you took Tiffany's life, you left her little girl, Jasmine, without a mother. She's an orphan now." Brooklyn watched as he prepared to strike the match. *Think fast!* "Without guidance and someone to teach her to avoid the mistakes of her mother, you've sentenced the child to a life of uncertainty."

"But isn't that what life is? An uncertain journey. No one gets a road map, do they?" He pulled open the door and struck a match, holding it in the air.

"Yes, they do! It's called the Bible!" she yelled after him

as he stepped outside, flicking the lit match to the ground after he stepped off the small porch.

Dear Lord, if that was just the wind earlier and no one is here to save me, please take me quickly.

A shadowy figure ran away from the building. Landon, who had been making his way through the graveyard with Heath while Jackson and his agents worked their way along the tree line to the opposite side of the building, darted toward the fleeing man.

As he drew close, Chastiser looked over his shoulder, his eyes widening, then took off to the left. Landon caught him by the arm, spun him around, drew back his fist and executed a right hook that would make any boxing professional proud.

Chastiser landed sprawled out on the ground, then rolled over and attempted to scramble to his feet. Landon grabbed him by the collar and pulled him upward.

Heath, who'd followed Landon, tried to loosen Landon's grip. "I'll take him from here."

Landon shook off the sheriff and leaned in close to his captive. "You better not have hurt her."

A smile spread across the older man's face. "Turn around. And look."

Landon glanced backward, then opened the fist that held Chastiser's shirt, dropping the man to the ground. The outside of the church was on fire, flames reaching past the windows on the right side close to the front doors.

Jackson ran over to them. "The tanker truck is only minutes away. We'll get her out of there."

Landon pressed past the agent. "Y'all take care of him." He jerked his head toward Chastiser, whom Heath was holding by the upper arm. "I'll get Brooklyn."

He raced toward the burning building before Heath or Jackson could stop him.

Agent Hawkins and the agent who had been on stakeout running the drone when they arrived, stood in the side yard, staring at the fire. What was wrong with these people? How could they just stand around knowing a woman was in danger inside the building?

Landon raced to the back of the building, looking for another entrance. The fire circled the building.

"We already looked," Jackson said from behind him. "While you were tackling Chastiser."

"I can't just stand out here and do nothing." Desperation clawed at him. "I've got to find a way inside."

"Except for a small gap, the fire circles the perimeter."

"Where? Where is a gap in the fire?" He took off around the opposite side of the building as hope surged inside him. Landon had to get to Brooklyn. She didn't need the risk of lung damage from smoke inhalation so close to her last exposure. Above all else, he could not stand the thought of her being inside, frightened and alone.

"The fire truck will be here any second. I can hear them coming," Jackson yelled, following him.

Midway along the left side of the building, there was approximately a five-foot gap in the flames. Block pillars balanced the church four feet above the ground, putting the bottom of the windows roughly eight and a half feet high. Two feet, four inches higher than Landon was tall.

"We think he may have missed this spot with the gasoline." Jackson walked several feet backward away from the window.

Landon walked closer and gasped. "The fire hasn't breached the building. If you'll give me a hand up, I can get to her."

The tanker truck pulled into the yard, the fire crew piling out and scrambling to connect the hoses.

Jackson put a hand on his arm. "They're here. They'll get the fire out quickly. Just give them a little time."

"I'm not waiting. It could still take them a while to get the fire out. I will not leave her in there alone and scared. Not when I'm right here and can get to her. Either give me a hand up, or I'll attempt to go through the fire at the back steps and try to break the back door down."

Jackson pursed his lips, nodded and stooped. With his fingers laced, he held his hand like a stirrup.

"Thank you." Landon grabbed a large rock before placing his right foot into Jackson's hand and reaching up for the edge of the window.

Jackson straightened, lifting Landon higher. He could see Brooklyn! Her eyes were closed and her head was tilted forward. *Lord, don't let me be too late.* He drew back the rock and rammed the glass as hard as he could. It shattered.

Brooklyn's head jerked upward, and her eyes turned in his direction.

She's alive! Thank You, Lord. Ignoring the fiery flames burning around them, he hit the glass until he'd cleared one pane. Then he tossed the rock to the ground.

"I need to go higher!" he yelled as the flames grew stronger.

Jackson grunted and lifted him another few inches. Landon reached his arm through the opening and unlocked the sash. He inched the window upward until there was a two-inch opening at the bottom, slipped his fingers under the sash and lifted the window as high as it would go. He pushed his upper body through the opening, bent at the waist and stretched his arms toward the floor. With his legs raised in the air, he slid downward until his hands connected with the floor, breaking his fall.

Brooklyn was yelling something, but he couldn't understand her as the blood in his body rushed to his head. Maneuvering his body, he pulled his legs through the window and dropped to the ground, coughing as smoke filled his lungs. Fire licked at the hem of his jeans. He pulled his leg close and slapped the fire out with his hands, ignoring the burning pain. Then he pushed to his feet and raced to Brooklyn's side.

"What are you doing? Why would you risk your life coming in here?" She coughed and shook her head. "I don't want you to die because of me."

Landon leaned in until he was face-to-face with her. "And I don't want to live without you."

Her eyes widened and her mouth formed an O. Tilting his head, he claimed her lips, savoring the kiss for the briefest moment. Pulling back, he dropped to his knees and untied her feet. Once they were free, he stood and worked on untying the rope that held her arms to her sides. Sweat ran into his eyes and he brushed it away with the back of his hand.

The double doors in the foyer burst open and two firefighters in full gear entered the front of the building, spraying water. Landon ignored them and continued working on loosening the knot. Finally, the rope dropped to the ground.

Brooklyn threw herself into his arms, burying her face in his neck. "I can't believe you came through fire for me."

"Whether you know it or not, there's nothing I wouldn't do to protect you. Now, let's get out of here." He scooped her into his arms.

"Put me down. I can walk."

"Not a chance." He raced down the aisle, past the two firefighters who were making their way around the room, searching the walls and ceiling for any sparks of flame. So far, the fire had not reached the inside of the building.

Running through the open double doors, he sprinted down the steps, jumping over the bottom two treads that had fire damage and dashing between the firefighters spraying water on the ring of fire circling the outside of the church. Landon didn't stop until he reached the spot where Jackson stood at the edge of the cemetery. He settled Brooklyn's feet on the ground, and the instant he straightened, she barreled into him, her arms wrapping around his waist, mumbling incoherently into his chest. He met Jackson's eyes. The agent smiled, turned and walked to meet Heath, who was making his way toward them.

Landon gently pried Brooklyn's arms loose and pulled back. He smiled and cupped her face with his hand, using his thumb to wipe away her tears. "Why don't we move a little farther away from the fire?"

She nodded. He draped his arm across her shoulders and guided her to the spot where Jackson and Heath stood talking several feet away. The men stopped talking as they walked up.

"Are you both okay?" Heath asked, his brow furrowed.

"Yes," they said in unison.

"Where's Chastiser?" Landon asked.

"He didn't get away, did he?" Brooklyn looked around as if she were searching for monsters in the dark. Landon pulled her closer to his side.

"No," Heath assured her. "He isn't going anywhere but the county jail. I left him handcuffed in the back seat of my patrol vehicle. Deputy Moore is standing guard."

Jackson touched Landon's arm. "The medic unit just arrived. It may be a good idea for you both to get checked out. They'll probably want to transport you to the hospital, as a precaution."

"I don't—"

"Yes, you do." Landon's lungs burned from the smoke he'd inhaled. He would not let her squirm her way out of being checked out. "I'll be right there with you. I'm sure it wouldn't hurt either of us to be given some oxygen to help clear our lungs."

Landon looked at the two men who had helped them so much the past week, his heart swelling with gratitude. "Thank you both for rescuing me today and getting me to Brooklyn before it was too late."

"All in a day's work," Jackson replied.

"We're thankful you're both safe." Heath nodded toward the medic truck. "Now, go."

Landon clasped Brooklyn's hand and walked over to the medic.

Fifteen minutes later, as the last flames were being extinguished, Brooklyn was seated in the back of the ambulance, wearing an oxygen mask. Landon grasped the grab bar to climb inside so they could be transported to the hospital, watching as the sheriff's cruiser drove by with Chastiser in the back seat.

If Brooklyn would allow it, Landon would spend the rest of his life helping her make happy memories to replace the memories of the nightmare Chastiser had put her through.

SEVENTEEN

The next morning, Brooklyn descended the stairs in Landon's home, ready for the workday. She hoped to finish early so she could check out a couple of rental properties. It was time she moved out on her own. Biting the corner of her lip as an army of butterflies and hummingbirds had a dance competition inside her stomach, she wondered where her host was. When they had left the hospital around midnight last night, Landon had said they would talk this morning. Was he going to tell her the kiss meant nothing? Had his actions the previous evening been an overexaggeration of emotions, brought on by his relief that she was alive?

The scents of bacon and eggs wafted to her. Quietly making her way through the front rooms, she entered the kitchen, pausing in the doorway to watch him flip an egg. He was dressed in his normal business attire, slacks and a button-down shirt, but something looked different. He appeared more relaxed.

"Perfect timing," he declared without looking up. "Breakfast is almost done. Come in and have a seat."

Heat crept up her neck. How had he known she was there? She hadn't made a sound.

Crossing to the cabinet, she removed a mug and filled

it with a splash of creamer and coffee. "Have you been up long?"

A blanket of awkwardness enveloped her, the same as it always did when she asked someone about the weather. Small talk had never been her forte.

"Almost an hour. Heath called to tell me he stopped by the garage this morning to get a look at my Jeep and talk to the mechanic. The brake lines had been cut. They also found a tracking device attached to the rear bumper."

She gasped. "That's how he kept finding us."

"Seems like it."

"How did he plant the tracker without being seen?"

"Who knows? He could have put it on when I left my garage door open. Or when he followed us to the motel." Landon plated the egg and handed it to her. "Toast and bacon are on the table. Eat while your egg is still hot."

"But—"

"You don't have to wait on me. Fried eggs taste better hot."

She giggled. "Okay, if you insist."

Settling in the chair at the kitchen table that had always been her chair when she'd lived with Lillian, she tucked into her breakfast. He had prepared her egg just the way she liked it, over medium with the yolk just runny enough to mop up the remnants with a slice of toast.

"Looks like you're enjoying your meal," Landon observed as he sat down beside her.

"It's good." She finished the last bite, placed her fork on her plate, plucked a paper napkin from the holder in the center of the table and wiped her mouth. "I don't think I realized before what a wonderful cook you are. The meat loaf you made at the cabin was the best I've ever eaten. I'm glad you didn't fool me into doing all the cooking."

"It was nice having you cook for me. Living alone for all of those years, it was either learn to cook or eat out for every meal, which could get expensive."

"I bet you had several women vying for your attention. Couldn't you convince any of them to cook for you?" She picked up her cup and swallowed a big gulp of coffee, the hot liquid burning as it went down. *Why did I ask that?* Brooklyn felt like she was back in middle school with her first crush.

A smile lifted one corner of his mouth and his eyes sparkled. Was he laughing at her? He finished his meal, leaving her in suspense. Once he was done, he gathered both plates, carried them to the sink and ran a little water over them.

Ugh. She'd gotten too personal. Brooklyn pushed back her chair and stood. She'd go to her office and prepare for the day, praying the awkwardness between them passed quickly. If it didn't, she didn't know what she'd do. Maybe she could open a private practice of her own. She'd always thought it might be nice to live in New England. She'd research areas and figure out the path for obtaining a license to practice in the state she chose.

"Are you no longer interested in the answer to your question?" Landon asked.

Brooklyn glanced up to see him leaned against the sink, drying his hands with a hand towel, watching her.

"I shouldn't have asked. It's none of my business."

"I beg to differ. It's definitely your business." He dropped the towel onto the countertop and walked toward her, never breaking eye contact.

Her heart raced. She bit the corner of her lip, fighting the urge to lick her lips. "Why?" she squeaked out.

He stopped in front of her and smiled. "Because I have

fallen hopelessly and completely in love with you. And I want there to be no secrets between us, ever."

Tears moistened her eyes.

"Why are you crying?"

"I never thought I'd experience what it was like to be in love." She laughed and brushed away the lone tear sliding down her cheek. "I was afraid the kiss yesterday was a reaction to the situation. I didn't dare hope it meant more."

He placed a hand on her cheek. "Oh, it did. It was much more than just a kiss. It was me giving my heart to you."

Landon buried his hands in her hair and lowered his head, claiming her lips in a kiss that erased any doubt of his feelings for her. She wrapped her arms around his waist, savoring the moment.

"Ahem…"

Brooklyn jumped at the sound of someone clearing their throat. Spinning around, she saw Marianne standing in the doorway. Her cheeks warmed.

"Yes, Marianne?" Landon inquired.

"Sorry to interrupt." A smile split her face. "As I was arriving just now, Mrs. Nabors pulled up. She asked to meet with Brooklyn. She said it was of utmost importance."

"Mrs. Nabors?" Landon glanced at Brooklyn, a raised eyebrow.

"Tiffany's caseworker." She moistened her lips. "Tiffany is dead. What would Mrs. Nabors have to discuss with me?"

"There's only one way to find out." Landon put his hand on her lower back and guided her to the rear hallway that was a shortcut to their offices, bypassing the reception area.

"Give us a few minutes to get settled and then you can send her in," Brooklyn said over her shoulder.

"Yes, ma'am." Marianne turned to do as instructed.

"Us?" Landon asked.

"Yes, us. Do you mind? I don't know that I can face whatever news Mrs. Nabors has to tell me today without you."

"Of course I don't mind. By your side is where I will always want to be." He opened his office door and escorted her inside. "We'll cut through here so she doesn't see us until you're ready for her."

His thoughtfulness warmed her heart. She never could have imagined the blessing that would result from Chastiser finding her again. As crazy as it sounded, she was thankful for all she'd been through, because it had helped her realize her feelings for the man beside her. With him as her champion and protector, there wasn't anything she couldn't face and overcome.

"Here's the letter Tiffany mailed to her mother the day before she was murdered." Mrs. Nabors leaned forward and handed the envelope to Brooklyn. "As you can see, it's notarized and is legally binding. It's up to you whether you want to accept the responsibility of raising her baby daughter."

Brooklyn pulled a sheet of folded notebook paper out of the envelope and opened it. Landon leaned over her shoulder.

I, Tiffany Carmichael, being of sound mind and body, do on this day write this, my last will and testament.

Someone had watched a few legal dramas, but Landon kept those thoughts to himself and kept reading.

To my mother, Laura Carmichael, I leave my eternal gratefulness for all the love and care she gave to me. I hope she can forgive me for not being the daughter I should have been. I'm sorry for the pain I brought her. I was trying to get my life together. I guess I didn't do it soon enough.

A wet spot—possibly a tear—had blurred the-*gh*.

As for my daughter, Jasmine, I name Brooklyn Thomas as her legal guardian. It is my desire that Brooklyn will adopt Jasmine and raise her as her own. My only requests are that she tell my daughter how much I loved her and that she allows my mother to stay in Jasmine's life.

Brooklyn placed the paper on her desk and leaned back in her chair. Landon could only imagine the thoughts racing through her head. He put his hand on her shoulder and squeezed, desperate to let her know she wasn't alone. No matter what choice she made, he would be supportive.

She glanced at him then turned her attention back to Mrs. Nabors. "Would it be possible for me to meet with Mrs. Carmichael to discuss this? I'd like to know her feelings on the matter."

"Yes." Mrs. Nabors nodded. "As a matter of fact, she wanted to talk with you as well. She's waiting in the car with Jasmine."

Everything was happening so fast. He wanted to speak up and say the meeting should be postponed for at least a day. Brooklyn had just survived multiple attempts on her life. She needed time to process everything. He tamped down his emotions. It wasn't his place to say anything. Brooklyn could make her own decisions.

"Would you please get her?" Brooklyn asked. "And then if you'll wait in the reception area, I'll let you know when I'm ready."

"Of course." Mrs. Nabors stood, nodded at them and exited the room.

"Wow." Landon sighed and walked around the desk and dropped into the recently vacated chair. "That was unexpected."

"Yes. It was." Brooklyn folded the paper and stuffed it back into the envelope, her hands shaking.

"If you need a few days to decide, no one is going to think badly of you. This is a lot to take in."

"I don't need time. I know what I want to do." She met his eyes, a solemn expression on her face. "I'm going to raise Jasmine, and I'm going to make sure she knows her mom loved her."

Her decision didn't surprise him in the least. Brooklyn had dedicated her life to being a servant to others, spreading God's love. Of course she'd take on the responsibility of raising a baby. He would have been shocked if her decision had been otherwise.

"Okay. I—"

"Look, if you have things to do in your office, I can finish this on my own."

On my own. Her words stung. Now that she was going to be a mom, was she planning to push him out of her life? What about their declarations of love? It suddenly hit him. When he'd professed his love for her, she hadn't declared her feelings for him. Was he wrong in thinking the feelings were reciprocated? *No.* She'd returned his kiss. He knew she loved him. And he would not let her drive him away. Landon pushed to his feet, keeping his emotions in check.

She stood, smoothed her skirt and offered him a forced smile—her lower lip quivering. "Thank you for everything. For your support just now and for saving me last night."

He dipped his head and walked toward the door that adjoined their offices, stopping when he drew even with her.

"Is that what you expect from me? That I'll walk away and leave you to handle all of this alone? What about our discussion in the kitchen earlier? Didn't you hear me tell you I love you?"

It tore him apart inside to bombard her with these questions, knowing she was likely battling a wave of emotions of her own, but he was in the fight of his life. He'd never dreamed he'd fall in love, and now that he had, he didn't want to lose her. *Lord, please, give me the strength to survive if she rejects me.*

"I heard you." Her voice cracked, and she pressed her lips together, staring at him for several long seconds.

He waited.

"Hearing you say *I love you* was the happiest moment of my life," she declared softly. "I first realized that I love you when you were trapped under the canoe and Chastiser was shooting at you."

"I was upset you didn't get away then, when he was distracted."

"I couldn't leave you."

"Then why are you trying to push me away now?" he demanded, not even trying to disguise the anger in his voice.

He'd never expected their first disagreement to happen the same day they declared their feelings for each other, but he would not walk away without trying to make her see his side of things.

"Because telling me you love me when I'm a single, unattached woman is one thing. I'm no longer unattached. I'm going to have a daughter, who will have to be a priority. My choices from here on out will be made based on what's best for her." She met his gaze, torture etched in her eyes. "Be honest. Do you really want to date a single mom?"

He took a step closer to her. "Honestly, no. I don't want to date a single mom."

Her shoulders slumped, and she shifted her gaze to the floor. He put a finger under her chin and lifted her face until their eyes locked.

"We didn't get to finish our conversation earlier. I left something unsaid. So, I'd like to say it now, if that's okay?"

"But Mrs. Nabors and Mrs. Carmichael are waiting."

"It won't take long."

She moistened her lips and nodded. "Okay."

"We've known each other for fifteen years. You're not some woman I just met who I want to date, intending to get to know her better."

Brooklyn's desk phone buzzed. He picked up the receiver. "Whatever it is, handle it." He started to replace the receiver, but then lifted it to his ear once more. "Tell Mrs. Nabors it will be a few more minutes. Sorry for her wait."

Landon dropped the receiver back onto the cradle and turned back to Brooklyn. Her mouth had formed an O. He had never interfered with anything concerning her clients or the running of her office, but this was important.

"You're right. I have no desire to *date* a single mom. But to be honest, I didn't *want* to date you."

Brooklyn's lips drooped at the corners—the O shape replaced by a frown.

This wasn't the setting he'd planned, but he rushed on, anyway. "I want to marry you."

Her eyes widened, and her mouth dropped open. Oh, how he loved her expressive face. He couldn't wait to spend a lifetime learning to read each expression.

He knelt on the ground in front of her. "I don't have a

ring. I haven't had time to go shopping. But I'm offering you my heart. And my eternal love and devotion. Brooklyn Hope Thomas, will you marry me?"

Laughter bubbled out of her as tears streamed down her cheeks. She knelt in front of him, clutching his hand. "People are going to think we've lost all common sense."

"Let them."

"They'll think… Oh, I don't even want to imagine what they will think." A pink hue colored her cheeks.

He squeezed her hand. "I don't care what anyone thinks. I want to know what you think. Will you marry me?"

"Yes. A thousand times, yes. I love you—" He pulled her into an embrace, kissing her soundly on the lips.

A baby's cries broke the silence. Landon pulled back and smiled. "I guess it's time we meet our daughter."

Brooklyn nodded, a radiant smile on her face. Landon's heart was so full. This was just the beginning, and their love would continue to grow with every passing day, month and year.

Thank You, Lord, for keeping her safe. I pray You will bless our union and that I will always be able to put a smile on her face.

EPILOGUE

Brooklyn pulled a wet wipe out of the diaper bag tucked under the table behind the ivory linen tablecloth. Turning nine-month-old Jasmine's face toward her, she wiped the sticky white icing off the child's rosy cheeks and hands and a small section of her curly black hair. Five months ago, if someone had told her she would be cleaning cake icing off her soon-to-be adopted daughter's face at her and Landon's wedding reception, she would not have believed them. But here she was, sitting at the head table, doing just that. She'd never thought she'd get married or have children. And now she had a husband and a daughter. She could almost hear Lillian saying, "God's plan is always greater than our own."

Jasmine pulled back from Brooklyn's grasp and shook her head. Then she touched the tips of her fingers together, signing the word *more*. "No, sweet pea. You can't have any more."

"Aw, come on, sweetheart," Landon said, coming up beside her. He scooped Jasmine out of her high chair and swung her around. "It's a special occasion. What's a little more cake going to hurt?"

Brooklyn smiled up at her handsome groom, his blue eyes shining. Jasmine giggled as he continued to dance with her. Brooklyn knew she was in trouble with these two. Jasmine had Landon wrapped around her tiny finger from the moment they had learned Tiffany had named Brooklyn as guardian of her baby girl.

Tiffany's mother, who'd had temporary custody of Jasmine since her birth and suffered from declining health, had been more than willing to have Brooklyn raise her granddaughter and allow her an opportunity simply to be the little girl's grandmother again. Since Mrs. Carmichael was the only known blood relative to the baby, Brooklyn had readily agreed…to everything. And Landon had been right there, helping every step of the way.

Within a week, he'd purchased an old commercial building downtown to house their agency so they could reclaim his entire house as their home. The commercial building had a second-floor loft apartment that he'd moved into until their wedding. He'd also hired a contractor and interior designer to knock out walls and construct a spacious play area, private bathroom, and small kitchenette between the rooms they had each chosen to use as their individual offices. This way, if one of them was tied up with a client, the other one could tend to Jasmine's needs. Even though Brooklyn had had reservations about the distractions having a nursery in such close proximity would cause—to both them and Jasmine—she had agreed to the project. And everything had worked out beautifully. But in this instance, she could not give in. More sugar being fed to a baby who had not been given any sweets prior to tonight would only be a recipe for disaster—for all of them.

"Not a chance. I'm sure Grammy wouldn't like the idea of pacing the floor all night with a cranky baby coming down from a sugar high."

"Sorry, kiddo. Mama said no."

Landon scrunched up his face, and Jasmine giggled. He kissed the top of her head.

"That's my sweet girl. Okay." He sat in the chair beside Brooklyn and balanced the little girl on his knee. "Let's practice. Dada…come on. You can say it. Dada."

Jasmine giggled and dived toward her. "Mama."

Brooklyn met Landon's eyes, tears of joy springing into hers. "Did she just say Mama?"

He nodded, a smile splitting his face. "That's what it sounded like."

She pulled her daughter to her chest and hugged her close. Brooklyn had never known she could love a child as much as she did the one in her arms. It didn't matter that she hadn't been the one to give birth to her. Jasmine was her daughter, and Brooklyn had loved her from the first moment she was placed in her arms.

Jasmine pulled back and repeated the sign for *more*. Brooklyn and Landon burst into laughter.

"Guess she was just buttering me up for more sweets." Brooklyn reached for her silverware and forked off a small bite of cake.

"Looks like it worked." Landon reached for the fork. "I'll feed her while you hold her. Maybe we can minimize the damage to your beautiful white gown."

"Sounds like a good plan." She settled Jasmine on her lap and faced her toward Landon.

Looking around the room, Brooklyn observed the small gathering of friends they had invited to share in their day. Heath and his wife, Kayla, sat at a table with Kayla's brother, Sawyer, and his wife, Bridget. Jackson Knight stood in the corner talking to Marianne and Dana.

Mrs. Carmichael came up to the table where Brooklyn and Landon sat with their daughter. "It was a beautiful ceremony. Thank you for inviting me, but it's getting late and I don't like to drive after dark. Would it be okay if I take Jasmine and head on home?"

"Of course." Brooklyn wiped Jasmine's mouth with a napkin.

Landon stood, and Jasmine held her arms up for him to take her. He lifted her into his arms, making it easier for Brooklyn to stand. She turned to Mrs. Carmichael. "Are you sure you don't mind watching her for a few days? We don't have to go—"

"Yes, you do, dear. It's your honeymoon."

"Well, just remember we're only going to Asheville. If you need us, we can be home in two and a half hours."

Mrs. Carmichael drew Brooklyn into a tight hug. "I never got to see my daughter get her life straightened out and have the life I dreamed of for her." The older woman's voice cracked. "And I think of you and Landon as my honorary children."

"Aww, we love you." Brooklyn returned the embrace. "We are *honored* to be considered your family. With neither of us having our mothers with us any longer, it is nice to have you stand in their stead."

Mrs. Carmichael pulled back, tears glistening in her eyes. "Well then, let me give you a bit of motherly advice. With a young child, you and your handsome new husband won't have much alone time. Enjoy your honeymoon. You're only going to be gone for three days. Jasmine will be fine. I'll take lots of pictures."

Landon leaned over and kissed the older woman's cheek. "Thank you, Momma Carmichael."

"Momma Carmichael. I like that." She smiled. "Now, give me my grandbaby and let me get her home. I'll probably have to put her in that baby bouncing chair with the colorful toys attached to it for her to burn to off some of that sugar y'all've been feeding her. Or she may not go to sleep tonight."

Brooklyn kissed the top of Jasmine's head, then kissed the cheek of the selfless woman who loved them all so much. "Thank you."

Landon slipped his arm around Brooklyn's waist as they watched the pair walk away. She leaned her head on his shoulder. "This has been the most perfect day."

The ceremony had been picturesque. They had gotten married in the church where Chastiser had tried to take her life, giving her a beautiful memory to outshine the darkest moment in her life.

"This is just the beginning. I will spend the rest of my life trying to make every day of your life better than the one before," Landon declared.

"I'm so thankful for you." She tilted her face upward. "I love you."

"I love you, too," he whispered just before his lips claimed hers.

The small crowd cheered, and her cheeks warmed.

Landon smiled and pulled back. "I don't know about you, my dear wife, but I'm ready to get out of here, too. Should we bid our guests farewell and get on the road?"

"Why, yes, husband, I believe we should."

Thank You, Lord, for blessing me with the family I never thought I'd have. I pray I never take my life for granted.

* * * * *

Dear Reader,

Thank you for reading Brooklyn and Landon's story. If two people ever deserved a happily-ever-after, it was these two. And it brought me great joy to write their love story. I hope you loved it as much as I do.

Chastiser was much harder to write. Sometimes I'd have to step away, do something else for a while, and then come back and tackle his scenes. However, writing his evil character was a constant reminder that we need to draw closer to the Light, spending extra time in His word, in times when life seems to be overshadowed by the darkness of the world.

Landon and Brooklyn drew strength from God, knowing He was always with them.

I would love to hear from you. Please connect with me at www.rhondastarnes.com and follow me on Facebook @rhondastarnesauthor.

All my best,
Rhonda Starnes